Complete Parenting

Also by Sirshree

Spiritual Masterpieces - Self Realisation books for serious seekers

The Secret of Awakening
100% Karma: Learn the Art of Conscious Karma that Liberates
100% Meditation: Dip into the Stillness of Pure Awareness
You are Meditation: Discover Peace and Bliss Within
Essence of Devotion: From Devotee to Divinity
The Supreme Quest: Your search for the Truth ends there where you are
The Greatest Freedom: Discover the key to an Awakened Living
Secret of The Third Side of The Coin
Seek Forgiveness & be Free: Liberation from Karmic Bondage
Passwords to a Happy Life: The Art of Being Happy in all Situations
The Light of Grace: Why Guru, God, Grace and You are one

Self Help Treasures - Self Development books for success seekers

The Source of Health: The Key to Perfect Health Discovery
Inner Ninety Hidden Infinity: How to build your book of values
Inner 90 for Youth: The secret of reaching and staying at the peak of success
The Source for Youth: You have the power to change your life
Inner Magic: The Power of self-talk
The Power of Present: Experience the Joy of the Now
You are Not Lazy: A story of shifting from Laziness to Success
Freedom From Fear, Worry, Anger: How to be cool, calm and courageous
The Little Gita of Problem Solving: Gift of 18 Solutions to Any Problem
Time Management: Highest use of your time to achieve your highest potential
Mind Your Brain, Master Your Life
Mastering the Art of Decision Making

New Age Nuggets - Practical books on applied spirituality and self help

The Source: Power of Happy Thoughts
Secret of Happiness: Instant Happiness - Here and Now!
Help God to Help You: Whatever you do, do it with a smile
Ultimate Purpose of Success: Achieving Success in all five aspects of life
Celebrating Relationships: Bringing Love, Life, Laughter in Your Relations
Everything is a Game of Beliefs: Understanding is the Whole Thing
Detachment From Attachment: Gift of Freedom From Suffering
Emotional Freedom Through Spiritual Wisdom
The Miracle Mind: How to master your mind before it masters you

Profound Parables - Fiction books containing profound truths

Beyond Life: Conversations on Life After Death
The One Above: What if God was your neighbour?
The Warrior's Mirror: The Path To Peace
Master of Siddhartha: Revealing the Truth of Life and After-life
Put Stress to Rest: Utilizing Stress to Make Progress
The Source @ Work: A Story of Inspiration from Jeeodee

Complete Parenting

How to raise your child with grace

A Happy Thoughts Initiative

Complete Parenting
How to raise your child with grace

By Tejgyan Global Foundation

Copyright © Tejgyan Global Foundation
All Rights Reserved 2019

Tejgyan Global Foundation is a charitable organization with its headquarters in Pune, India.

Published by WOW Publishings Pvt. Ltd., India
First edition published in January 2019

This book is a translation of the original Hindi book *Bacchon Ka Sampurna Vikas Kaise Karen.*

Copyrights are reserved with Tejgyan Global Foundation and publishing rights are vested exclusively with WOW Publishings Pvt. Ltd. This book is sold subject to the condition that it shall not by way of trade or otherwise, be lent, resold, hired out, or otherwise circulated without the publisher's prior written consent in any form of binding or cover other than that in which it is published and without a similar condition including this condition being imposed on the subsequent purchaser and without limiting the rights under copyright reserved above, no part of this publication may be reproduced, stored in or introduced into a retrieval system, or transmitted, in any form, or by any means, electronic, mechanical, photocopying, recording or otherwise, without the prior written permission of both the copyright owner and the above-mentioned publisher of this book. Any person who does any unauthorized act in relation to this publication may be liable to criminal prosecution and civil claims for damages.

CONTENTS

Preface	Every Child Can Touch the Sky	07

NINE POWERFUL MESSAGES   11

1.	Improve Yourself Before Improving Your Child	13
2.	Every Child Can Become a Super Hit Film	18
3.	Your Presence Rather Than Your Presents is The Best Gift	23
4.	Parents Should Become Sculptors of Their Kids	27
5.	Raw Child, Good Child, True Child	29
6.	Parenting Styles	35
7.	Understand Your Child's Definition of Love	40
8.	Qualities Required in Parents	43
9.	How do Children Learn?	49

NINE POSITIVE STEPS   53

10.	Give The Right Training to Your Kids	55
11.	Give Unconditional Love	62
12.	The Mantra for A Happy Family: Good Communication	65

13.	Open Up, Blossom, and Play with Children	72
14.	How to Bring About Complete Development of Children	77
15.	Don't Say Sometimes 'Yes' And Sometimes 'No'	81
16.	The World Needs Well Trained Children	84
17.	Children Should Understand the Real Meaning of Failure	89
18.	Good Character in Youth is the Need of Today	95

ERADICATE THESE FOUR NEGATIVES — 101

19.	Problems Related to Children	103
20.	Anger Related to Children	110
21.	Parenting Myths	114
22.	Doubts and Queries Regarding Children (FAQs)	122

THREE FINAL IMPORTANT SUGGESTIONS — 139

23.	Importance of Teachers in A Child's Life	141
24.	Importance of Prayer and Meditation in Children's Life	150
25.	Importance of Becoming 'Bright' Parents	155

Preface
EVERY CHILD CAN TOUCH THE SKY
and not become a bonsai

The impressions formed in the womb play a very important role in shaping a child. Most of us are aware of this fact. However, the work of creating positive impressions should not stop after the child is born. This is the way to help every child develop into an ideal human being.

You may have heard many people saying, "Children teach us a lot." It's true. Children are so innocent that just by looking at them we learn what it means to live in the present. Every little child lives without any burdens or thoughts and is always happy. They are not worried about tomorrow or even the next moment. They always live in the now. To live happily in the present moment is the most important thing. This is what we can learn from them.

Many parents feel the upbringing of their children as a burden because they raise their children with the thought: "This is *my* kid." While the truth is, the child has only come into this world through them.

Two trains may run together on parallel tracks but their journeys are different. Much in the same way, your child is on its journey alongside yours. *Allow* them to be on their journey. You can only support them and walk by their side. Every child born on Earth has their own purpose and their own lessons to learn. They are here to know themselves fully, to discover their infinite and divine nature. They are here to fully open up, blossom, and play this divine game being played on Earth. We, as parents, only need to help them so that they become capable of living a wonderful life. We should form such impressions and educate our children in a way that would make them a boon for the society. Let's see how we can do that with the help of a little story.

> An old man was once cleaning his grounds and digging a pit. A young man from his neighborhood was passing by and asked him why he was digging the pit.
>
> There was a shine in the old man's eyes as well as his words. "I will sow a seed in it, add fertilizer, and then water it every day. The seed will sprout and grow into a sapling. I'll protect it to ensure that it doesn't get damaged by excessive winds or rains. The sapling will develop into a plant and eventually grow into a big tree. This tree will then provide shade and fruit to all the people passing by."
>
> On listening to the old man's thoughts, the young man's curiosity rose even further. "This process will take years and, pardon me, but you're already quite old. What will *you* gain from it?"
>
> The old man smiled. "I am not doing this with any expectations for myself. I only wish for this seed to blossom and bear fruit. I want it to be able to grow and express its true nature."

These words of the old man are worth pondering over for every parent. Because in these words lies the secret of how to help our children achieve complete development and why.

Many seeds get the ground to germinate but not the other essential requirements, due to which they cannot develop into a fully-grown tree but become a bonsai. Bonsai is a miniature tree which only resembles a big tree and gives little fruits but no shade. It's a tree whose growth has been restricted and capability has been hampered. We too have some plants in our home that have the ability to touch the sky. Are we by any chance turning them into a bonsai?

Development of only one aspect of life is not complete development. These plants should grow, rise up, and become magnificent trees in all aspects of life. Every child has the capacity to become a great person. This possibility lies hidden within them right from birth. Parents only need to have faith, the foresight, and the ability to take right decisions at the right time.

We all had dreams during our childhood. Similarly, our kids are dreaming today. Their worlds of dreams are like butterflies with colorful delicate wings. We as parents need to ensure not to break these wings. Their twinkling eyes full of curiosity should not fill with darkness by our use of force and anger. Allow these butterflies to fly, play, dance, and experiment. Do not tie their wings. They are soft and gentle. Even your harsh voice frightens them. Nurture them with love and care.

Every child should become a great tree and not a bonsai. This is the goal of complete development of children. Some points, which are crucial, are purposely repeated in this book. Internalize the message of this book and utilize it to its maximum. It will help you raise children that have cultivated great virtues and attained their maximum potential. This is Complete Parenting.

*Don't postpone to tomorrow
what can be done for your child today.
Because then half your time tomorrow
will be spent on doing
what you were supposed to do today.
Thereby, you won't be able to give the time and love
you wanted to give to your kids,
and they may indulge in activities
that could be harmful for them.*

Nine Powerful Messages

1. Improve yourself
2. Teach through stories
3. Converse in the right way
4. Be a sculptor
5. Understand your children
6. Know yourself
7. Read your kid's dictionary
8. Balance between love and discipline
9. Be an ideal for your kids

1
IMPROVE YOURSELF BEFORE IMPROVING YOUR CHILD
One but a lion

If you want your child to become a lion or a lioness, you will have to become one first.

One day, all animals of the jungle had got together and were chatting with each other. The topic had moved on to their young ones. The fox said it had two young ones. The elephant said it had three. The bear said four. When the lioness was asked, "How many kids do you have?" she said, "One." Some of the animals remarked, "Just one?" She replied with pride, "Yes, just one. But he's a *lion!*"

What do you want to make your children? Have you been thinking on this? Lots of parents want their children to become a Swami Vivekananda or a Rabindranath Tagore or a Bill Gates or a Shivaji.

But if you want your child to become Shivaji, then first you will have to become Jijamata (his mother, historically credited with his success). You will have to cultivate the qualities of Jijamata so that you can give birth and raise a Shivaji. You will need to inculcate the qualities of a lioness. Only then will your child become a lion.

Every parent wants to do everything for their child because the child is their dream. They want to give the very best education to them. They want their child to grow into an intelligent, polite, cultured, and great individual. They want their kid to make a name for their family. Such parents are ready to do anything for their kids. However, do they follow the right path toward this purpose?

If parents wish that their children should fulfill their expectations, are they giving them all that the children need? Are they creating the right environment for them to grow and blossom?

Here the first important question that arises is: "Do we *communicate* with our children?" Communication does not mean just talking to them but it also means exchange of thoughts, appreciating them at the right time, and giving the right punishment or forgiving them for mistakes made. Forgiving does not mean forgetting their mistakes. It means making them aware of their mistakes and giving them suggestions and guidance so that they don't make the same mistakes again.

For example, if some object happens to break when our kid was handling it, our first question is: "*Why* did you do this? Why don't you *listen*? When will you *grow up*? *Why* did you break it?" Does the child have an answer to these "why's"? Did he really want to break that object? It happened unwittingly, so how can he answer why he broke it? But if he gets punished for it, he says his foot slipped or the other kid pushed him (which is probably a lie) and that is why the object fell and broke. This one question by the parents teaches a new lesson to the child that if something breaks or any such mistakes occur, he can just make up something or put the blame on others, so as to escape punishment. Gradually, he begins to blame others for everything, which then continues throughout his life. He has developed a tendency or pattern of blaming others, which is called the *Blamer Pattern*. Parents need to take care to avoid the formation of such tendencies.

While dealing with children, we should remember that they too have the right to make mistakes. But our focus should not always be on their errors. They should not be frequently reminded of their slip-ups. Some parents keep rebuking their kids saying, "Yesterday you broke a glass, what are you going to break today?" They also tell their guests, "Our son is very naughty. He has broken all the glass windows in the neighborhood." By narrating these blunders, what image of your child are you presenting to others? Where is your focus?

The more you focus on their mistakes, the more errors they will make. On the other hand, when they do something nice, is your focus on their good deeds? If you can do this, it will prove to be very beneficial for the child. When the child gets good grades in a test, you must be generous in your appreciation and encouragement. You can say something like, "How intelligent my child is! He studied very hard and hence got such good grades. If he studies more, I'm sure he will top the class." If a child has won a race, praise her by saying, "What fabulous running! One day you will definitely become a good athlete."

If your attention is in the right direction, the child will do even better. This is because you focused on and gave attention to their good qualities and good work. Never scold the child on their mistakes. Instead ask, "What did you learn from this mistake?" When parents point out the error in appropriate words, the child certainly learns from it. Even using the right words with your child has a great impact on them.

For instance, a kid is speaking with his friend in a very loud voice. Hearing it, his father comes out from his room and screams, "Why are you shouting? You disturbed my sleep." Now the child thinks, "If I am shouting, then what is dad doing? He too is shouting at me." Hence, we have to be very careful about what words we use with our child. Instead of saying, "Don't shout," we can say, "Speak softly." Instead of saying, "Don't slam the door," we can say, "Close the door gently."

Such positive words steer your child away from negative thoughts. Every parent wishes that their children should not become negative. But always keep in mind that the children should be able to express negative feelings, if they have them. They have the right to express those feelings.

For example, a small child is crying. If he wants something, he will cry and ask for it, or he will ask for it with irritation. He is allowed to do so. Ask the child what happened and what he wants. This will enable him to express what he is feeling. Give him the opportunity to do so, rather than telling him to shut up. Otherwise, one day he will blast and start breaking things around. When attention is not paid to the feelings of children, they develop the *Blaster Pattern*.

If we can express negative feelings such as anger and irritation, then even kids have the right to do so. If the child is very young, how will he express his unhappiness and irritation? How will he communicate with his parents? Therefore, first ask him, "Why are you doing this?" Or pay attention and listen to what he has to say or give him something that he wants, and then try to discuss with him in a nice manner. If required, exercise some authority. Finally, give him enough time and understand his negative emotions, and then try to help him to come out of those feelings.

Some parents always stop children in whatever they are doing. They say, "Don't do this… don't do that… don't climb the window… don't shout… don't cry… don't come here… don't go there…" Children do not understand the meaning of this constant hindering from the parents. So, don't tell them what *not* to do, but what to do.

You may have observed that when a child is told, "Don't do this and don't do that," he asks, "Then what should I do?" This is because every kid wants to do something. Therefore, whenever a child asks, "Daddy, shall I do this?" never say "no" to him right away. Instead say, "Certainly. But it will be better if you would rather do that way, because it will help you achieve what you want." This will increase the child's self-confidence, which will help him throughout his life.

While dealing with children,
we should remember that they too
have the right to make mistakes.

2
EVERY CHILD CAN BECOME A SUPER HIT FILM
Use stories to teach your kids

A child can become a super hit film,
which can create yet another super hit film.

Every child can become either a super hit film or a flop. It all depends on the parents what they want their child to be. If they want their kid to be a super hit, they need to play the role of a director, a story writer, a producer, a photographer, a makeup artist, a musician, and a choreographer. Only then can a super hit film be made, which going ahead can make another such super hit movie.

A movie in the external world can become a big super hit but it cannot make another super hit movie on its own. But a child can. The only condition is that the child should get parents who can play the role of a director in the right manner.

If parents have time for their kids but not wisdom, then all that the children receive from their parents is fear and wrong beliefs. Due to these beliefs, the kids live a constricted life. If you really want your child to become fully prepared before they step into the world, then you will need to work on them like a super hit film and you need to develop them to their fullest. When this film will be released, people will wonder how an individual can have so many amazing qualities!

Role of a director

The director of a super hit movie or play handles all the actors together on one stage and ensures no conflicts occur between them. He also makes sure that all actors play their role in the best manner. There is a different role for every actor but the stage is the same for all of them. The director knows how to control each actor, how to communicate with them, who gets upset when, and who gets terrified on stage or in front of the camera. Due to this knowledge, he knows when they need guidance and how to guide every actor smoothly and correctly.

The role of the director is mostly to guide. He knows who should be with whom, which actor should be placed with which other actor, so that there is peace on the set, and the movie or play will develop satisfactorily.

Parents are just like a director. They too need to manage all the family members together. Because at home, along with them, there are kids, siblings, grandparents, and sometimes even neighborhood kids. Parents take care to ensure all of them live together in peace under one roof. It is only by conducting themselves in the right way with their kids that parents can play the role of a good director.

Importance of stories

Kids listen to stories very attentively. They love stories more than Diwali or Christmas vacations. Hence, for them you have to sometimes play the role of a storywriter too. The job of the storywriter here is to tell a story. As you communicate more and more with your kids and tell them stories, they start opening up and feeling safe with you.

Suppose, a kid has developed a bad habit or has the habit of lying.

Then, through a story, you can try to convey how bad habits and speaking lies ruins one's life. By narrating a story that illustrates your point, you may say that there was a boy who used to lie and how his lies one day landed him in serious trouble. Thereafter how he got rid of this habit and how his life then became happy and he became successful.

You can explain all of this to your kid with the help of a story. Children pick up a lot from such stories because they learn more with their right brains as compared to the left brain. Hence, it is essential to teach them using visual cues, pictures, or imagination. This is where stories too come in and kids *want* to hear stories. That is why parents need a little bit of training, a little bit of practice, and to read some books, and search some stories. This will help them to choose and narrate the right stories to their kids in order to eradicate any bad habits that they have. If a kid always avoids work, he can be instructed by narrating a story of a man who was lazy. From this story, he will learn how to get rid of his laziness. Thus, to eliminate a bad habit in a child, it is parents who have to make the effort.

Sometimes, you may bring your kids such toys and books that will develop their right brain. Specific type of toys can be helpful in boosting the self-confidence of your child. There are various toys, games, and books that can aid in their growth. Cultivate the habit of reading in your kids. Many types of books are available for children to read, which they can easily read themselves and understand. Don't think, "They are just kids! How will they understand?" Kids can comprehend a lot but you need to choose the right books for them.

Which videos should you give your kid to watch? Which books should you give? What is it that their brain accepts easily? Which bad things are they attracted to? You will come to know all of these by talking to your child. By having good conversations with your kids, you can create a platform of friendship with them. This will enable them to openly tell you everything that is happening with them. If there is something wrong occurring in school or with other friends, they will talk to you about it and you are then able to guide them suitably on the matter. If parents and kids have such friendship and good communication, then these kids will soon grow up and create a highly evolved world. They will be able to work toward their inner and outer growth and progress.

If you can be a story writer, then your kids can develop all good qualities. When children are told stories that inspire, they listen with rapt attention. Every event and everything that happens in the story leaves a lasting impression in their brains. Thus, with tales and fables, you can easily teach your kids just about anything.

Role of a photographer

In order to make a film, you need a director, a story writer, a producer, and a financer. Along with these, there is a photographer who enhances the confidence of the actor and tells him which scene he did best. The makeup artist does the right makeup, which also boosts the actor's confidence. The choreographer demonstrates how the actor has to dance.

In the same way, parents also need to play the role of a photographer who shows the child how he used to study in school and in which events he used to participate. They should show their kid his photo album from childhood. "Look, when you were little, you had got first prize." If the kid had performed on stage for a school function, he should be shown those pictures and videos. By seeing those, his confidence rises knowing that he has already done all those things. He feels, "I have already been on stage, so I can go on stage again."

It can be said that the role of a photographer was performed properly only if your kids get a boost in their confidence. Likewise, it can be said that the role of a choreographer was done correctly when you demonstrate to your kids the qualities you want to see in them and how certain activities should be carried out, and then the kids are able to do it exactly in the same manner.

You need to become like a child—good, raw, and truthful.
To do so, you need the strength and the intellect
to accept the new.

3
YOUR PRESENCE RATHER THAN YOUR PRESENTS IS THE BEST GIFT

Communicate in the right manner with your child

While training your children, never give the excuse of "I don't have time." Because you too have the same amount of time that Edison had. Recognize the value of time. The childhood of your kid will never come back.

More important than giving expensive toys and clothes to your kids is giving them time.

Give your children enough time, so that they feel they are important to their mom and dad. When children say something, listen to them attentively. You will see enthusiasm on their faces. Look them in the eye while listening to them. You will see their love. When the child is saying something and the parent is watching television or reading a newspaper, then attention is not paid to the child. This makes the child feel, "I am telling something with so much interest and seriousness, but they are not even paying attention to me." Such children feel isolated. Hence, pay attention to everything that the child has to say, support them, and respond to them, so that they feel that their mom and dad are always with them and they are not alone. This increases their morale and confidence.

Those who want their son to become a Shivaji, will have to become Jijamata first. It is well-known how much time Jijamata gave Shivaji, due to which Shivaji could became a king. He fought against the Mughals and was able to achieve freedom of his kingdom at the age of 16. Jijamata was always with him. She encouraged and inspired him at every step, due to which Shivaji rose to such heights as to become an Emperor or *'Chatrapati.'* Jijamata never told him, "You practice sword-fighting and I'll go home." She was constantly with him and always boosted his self-confidence.

If children are to progress, we have to walk with them. We have to give them time and space. Giving only time is not sufficient; we have to give them space as well. 'Giving space' means sometimes we need to leave them alone to do some things. Many parents don't allow their children to go out alone. The child wants to do something. He or she has certain qualities that they can manifest by going somewhere else. But some parents insist that their kids always remain in their sight. Due to excessive attachment, they don't send them to another city for further studies. When the time comes for them to go to college, they get them enrolled in a nearby college. If the child is a bit late in coming home from school or college, they get extremely worried. This demoralizes the child. It becomes difficult for the kid to take decisions.

If children have such parents and are raised in this way right from childhood, how will they open up and bloom? How can they openly communicate what they want to do and what they want to become? Hence, it is very important for children to always have free communication with their parents, because this is the one quality that helps love to grow in this relationship. If we don't inculcate this habit in our kid during childhood, they won't be able to talk to elders openly and remain scared even on growing up. They consider themselves to be inferior to others and loses their self-confidence. In spite of having good qualities, they are unable to express those, and remain behind throughout their lives. These are the individuals whom parents have always rebuked during their childhood saying,

"Keep quiet! Don't say anything." If they made a mistake, the mother had said, "Let Daddy come home. I'll tell him what you did and he will teach you a lesson."

What image of the father did the mother give to the child? The child thinks daddy is going to punish him and hence does not want to face him. This affects their relation. In childhood itself, if daddy's image is that of Hitler, then what will their relationship be? Thus, it is crucial to give such an image of dad and mom to the children that they would wish to be like them on growing up. Parents should be an inspiration for the child.

If we want cooperation from our child, how should our communication be with them? How should we talk to them? How should we ask them or tell them? It is essential to understand these aspects. Kids will cooperate when asked in the right manner. For example, when a father tells his young kid to fetch a glass of water, how did he say it? Is his tone like giving an order or is it said in a loving manner? If we are directly ordering, how will the child cooperate? He may still fetch the water, to which the father says, "Good Boy." After some time, the kid is playing and happens to break something. The father yells, "What did you do?! Are you an idiot? You are a *bad* boy!" The child thinks that just a while ago he was a good boy, now how did he become a bad boy? The child is too young and cannot understand why his dad is saying two different things. The kid has made a mistake, so what? Did he plan and do it? But parents think he is doing it deliberately. They not only think so but also say it. They say such words to kids that are not appropriate for them.

It is our responsibility as parents to learn the right way to communicate with our children right from their childhood. Kids should be able to openly convey to their parents about what happened or what is happening with them. In the same way, parents should also be able to talk openly with their kids. They should be able to convey how it troubles them when he gets into trouble. You may think that children won't be able to understand. But how much they understand will surprise you. Hence the importance of establishing a two-way communication right from childhood.

When faced with some problem, people think, "What do we do now? Let's sit together and solve the problem." However, the preparation for such communication should have been done much earlier. When is the right time to start exercising? On falling sick or much earlier? If we begin early, then we won't fall sick, and even if we do, we will recover quickly. Similarly, communication with children is a habit that should be formed right from the beginning, so that no rifts develop in this precious relation. Even if some misunderstanding occurs, it should be cleared through communication. Therefore, the platform for communication should be established early on.

We are part of the same family. Each one of us is a well-wisher of the others. All of us want happiness. Then why do disputes occur? Why does antagonism develop? On analyzing, you will find that the reason is the lack of communication between parents and kids. When communication begins, then the habits and patterns that have formed in each other will begin to break automatically. The ego pattern in the father makes him think, "How can I talk with my child? How can I take his advice?" This pattern breaks when communication begins. If the child has fear pattern, that too will disappear.

Positive words have vibrations which can make one healthy. Hence, always use optimistic and inspiring words with your children.

4

PARENTS SHOULD BECOME SCULPTORS OF THEIR KIDS

Two points for wealthy parents

Parents' money quite often becomes a curse for their kids. This is because these children avoid hard work and miss out on the opportunity to explore their qualities and talents.

It is observed nowadays that when people meet and chat, they tell each other, "Our kids have become really stubborn. They don't listen to anybody. Why do they behave in this manner?"

While saying this, have we ever thought who is responsible for this? If we really reflect on it, the painful answer that would arise would be that we ourselves are responsible for it.

Today's world has become highly materialistic with all its various temptations. We want all the comforts and luxuries without putting in much effort, and that too as soon as possible. Most often we don't hesitate in choosing any way that may seem possible to fulfill our desires. So, what are our children learning from us today? What do they see in us? They see us exactly as we are! We don't teach this to our kids but only by seeing us and listening to us, they automatically learn things.

If kids obstinately demand something, parents immediately fulfill their desire without even thinking whether the desired object is even required or not. Parents think "My kids should have all the pretty and expensive things so that we can show off in our friend circle." However, such children end up becoming stubborn and careless squanderers. After growing up, these pampered kids are unable to face any change in their circumstances. They then adopt just about any way possible to fulfill their needs and desires.

That is why today's youth doesn't understand the difference between good and bad. If they don't have something, they feel they are lacking and also feel embarrassed in front of their friends. "What would my friends think of me?" This question haunts their minds. Money, which is actually a medium for prosperity and happiness, ends up becoming their final goal. If these kids were taught in their childhood the virtues of patience and spending wisely, they would become great citizens in the future.

Parents' money quite often becomes a curse for their children. This is because these kids avoid hard work and miss out on the opportunity to explore their qualities and talents. They never get to taste the wonderful flavor of hard work. They never feel true hunger because they are served before they get hungry. Thus, the kids of rich parents mostly prove to be unfortunate in the race of life. They are unable to do even a minor thing for themselves. They remain ignorant of so many critical aspects of life, such as, what is the challenge of life? How to awaken our dormant powers? What are our needs and what are our desires? What should be our goal?

If children learn the importance and the difference between a need and a want, then they can also understand the difference between good and bad in all areas of life. If you want to become a sculptor of your child's life, you first need to sculpt yourself. Only then will you be able to sculpt and mold your child into a good human being. Only *you* can do this. And it's only *you* who have to do this.

5
RAW CHILD, GOOD CHILD, TRUE CHILD
Know thy child

First you make habits. Then habits make you.
Hence, inculcate the habit of developing
new and positive qualities in your children.

Every child is raw, good, and true when they are born. Let us understand these qualities in detail.

Raw child

When the child is very young and raw, parents need to play the role of a potter. Just as a potter creates a pot using a lump of soft clay, you have to do the same for your child. A potter can mold the soft clay into any shape he wishes to. He first puts the clay on the moving wheel. He then supports it from the inside to turn it into a small pot. Thereafter, he uses a stick and taps with his hand the little pot from the outside, to transform it into a beautiful large vessel. Subsequently, he places this vessel in the fire, which hardens it. Only then it becomes a container that is capable of holding water.

The same is the process of raising a child. When a child is young and malleable, you need to nurture them with your love in this ever-changing, revolving world. When they are growing up, sometimes you have to tap them or use discipline to keep them on track. When a child grows into a young adult, they need to be tested in the fire of various circumstances and certain situations, so that they become capable of holding the water of wisdom.

Good child

A child is always good. They always think good. When they are little, they see everything with the same eye of wonder. Everything appears new and good to them. That's why they want to touch everything and feel everything with their hands.

The contrast mind—the mind that always judges, compares, and labels everything as "good" or "bad"—is not yet formed in the child. Later on, the parents make them aware of what is good and what is bad.

True child

A young child is free from deceit, which means they are truthful. They always say whatever they want to say. They speak exactly what they feel. Hence, when they say something, listen to them with full attention.

There are some habits that should be inculcated in a child right from childhood when they are raw and receptive. These habits would be those that are going to be beneficial for them in the future. "First man makes habits. Then habits make the man." Hence, why not sow the seeds of right habits and virtues in your child that will help them in their upcoming years? If this is done, your child is going to become a good person.

If your child is going to be good, then they are going to be truthful as well. Both these qualities go hand in hand. All parents want their kids to do well in their lives and bring a good name to their families. They want them to study well and attain the heights of success, but all of this can happen only if parents give something from their side first. This includes undisturbed time, actual attention, security, and unconditional love.

Bright parents are able to give these gifts to their children. What does 'Bright' parents or 'Bright' individual mean here? A 'Bright' individual or 'Bright' householder is one who sincerely fulfills all their worldly responsibilities while walking the spiritual path and working on attaining the ultimate goal of life. The ultimate goal of each and every one of us is to realize our true divine self, get established in that state, and express our divine qualities. 'Bright' parents are two such individuals who are on this sacred path and have attained the higher understanding of every aspect of life, including parenting, by listening to or reading the teachings of a true spiritual master. As a result, they possess certain qualities which make them role models for their kids. They always keep in mind the following five points for their kids:

1. **Never compare your child with others**

    The first thing that Bright parents keep in mind is that every child is unique and hence different from others. It also means that every child has some unique qualities and skills. Hence, Bright parents never compare their children with others.

    Even if the neighbor's kid got 90 percent marks, whereas their kid got only 60, yet Bright parents do not compare their child with the other, because they know that even if their child did not achieve good marks, but he or she is good in sports. Every body-mind is different and proficient in different fields. Bright parents encourage and praise their kids for the qualities they possess.

2. **The child learns to ask**

    The second point that Bright parents recognize is that

children are always going to desire and ask for something. Also, whatever they want at any given time, they want more of it. And why shouldn't they? Kids have the right to ask for more. We adults too want more of everything—more time, more money, a more luxurious car, a more spacious house, and so on. Then why can't our kids ask for more? When children start asking in this way and putting forth their desires, the quality of 'how to ask' develops in them. They learn how to talk and deal with the family members so as to achieve a successful give and take. This trains them to become enterprising and able to deal with people when they step out in the world. They also learn how to become good negotiators because they learn from their parents: "Ask and you shall receive." Bright parents teach them how to ask and negotiate in the right manner.

3. A child has the right to make mistakes

The third important point that Bright parents understand is that their children will make mistakes, and they have the right to do so. Adults make mistakes too, so why can't kids? They are actually learning something from those mistakes.

Most parents rebuke their kids for any slip-ups. "How can you make such a huge blunder!" This affects the morale of the kids. However, Bright parents know that children not only make mistakes but also learn to correct them. If they fall down, they learn to stand up again. Bright parents don't laugh or get irritated at the errors of their kids. But they always ask them this one thing: "What did you learn from this mistake?" The lesson that children learn from a mistake stays with them throughout their lives. In this way, even a few positive word from the parents can encourage kids to move and progress ahead.

4. **Every child expresses their feelings differently**

   The fourth point that Bright parents know is that sometimes kids express themselves in a negative manner, and it is necessary for them to do so. If a little child does not like something, how will they convey that? They may cry and scream or become sad and sit quiet.

   So, why shouldn't they do this? Is it wrong to cry? If kids want to express their discontent, they will cry. What else can they do? Grown-ups can express their discontent in words, but a small child can only express in this manner. Bright parents are aware that by acting out, the kids are just trying to express their feelings. Hence, they deal with them coolly and calmly. They find the cause and the solution to their displeasure, soothe their anger, and shoo away their sorrow.

5. **A child learns to present their thoughts in the right manner**

   The fifth point that Bright parents understand is that sometimes children can say "no" to something. And if they do, what's the problem? If adults can say no to certain things, then so can kids. Bright parents know that sometimes their kids are going to refuse to do something, and they also understand why it is necessary for kids to do so. By saying no, they are developing certain qualities, such as how to be assertive, how to debate, how to present their point properly, how to explain their perspective, and how to refuse things that they don't want or need.

All Bright parents are aware of these five crucial points and that is why they neither compare their child with others, nor do they suppress them in any way. They know that their child is going to make some mistakes but also learn from it. Kids can say "no" to things that they don't like, and this will help them in the future. Bright parents teach their children those things that help them become good human beings and good citizens. So, are we too becoming Bright parents?

Some parents demand so much from their kids, but are they providing all that the kids need in order to fulfill their demands? If we want to become ideal parents, we will have to learn some things, get rid of some old habits and perspectives, and adopt some new ones.

When you see a child, you want to pick them up and hug them. This is because in a child, the experience of divinity and true love is in an awakened state.

6
PARENTING STYLES
Ten Qualities of Bright Parents

Complete parents know that the child has come into this world through them; they do not own the child. Children are God's property and not the means to fulfill their own desires.

There are six kinds of parents. Or we can call it as six styles of parenting. Let us learn the characteristics of each so that you can identify your style of parenting.

1) Slave Parents

Such parents are blinded by attachment and simply don't know where the well-being of their child lies. They are also not aware of how the child can develop and progress, and how he or she can attain happiness and good health. These parents keep their child in their own world and meet all the demands of the child.

In this type too, there are two kinds of parents. Some parents consider their son to be everything and deem their daughter to be subservient to her brother. Some parents treat their daughter as everything, and everyone in the house caters to her and her tantrums.

Such kids initially may or may not listen to their parents but get spoilt on growing up. They get all their whims and fancies fulfilled by their parents. This affection of the parents becomes poison for the kids in the long run.

Some of these kids don't heed their parents at all and continue to torment them until their demands are met. Such parents feel quite distressed and even fearful of their kids.

2) Overprotective Parents

Some parents are overly concerned and always worry about their child getting hurt or lost. Consequently, they become over-protective and do not allow their children to be independent.

3) Busy Parents

If both parents go out for work, they cannot give their children as much time as they should. Some parents are always partying, attending events, or holidaying. When available at home, they are quick to punish the child for every mistake because they don't have the time or patience to listen to them. These children become disheartened and depressed. They may fall into bad habits or lead an isolated life.

4) Self-centered Parents

Such parents think only about themselves and do not care about their kids at all. They make the children work for their own pleasure and comfort. Some parents treat their kids as an investment. They have no love for them but take care of them only because they think that these children will look after them on growing up. Such parents are not very common but they do exist.

5) Strict Parents

Such parents always get angry and reprimand their children for every little slip-up. They never listen to them and want to discipline them only through anger. They don't realize that when these children grow up, they too will behave with their own kids and with other people in the same manner. The heart of such children gets closed. They are never able to understand what love is even after growing up.

6) Complete Parents

'Bright' parents are Complete parents. They always want their children to progress and help them in every way to make that possible. They teach them what is the highest they can achieve according to their inherent talent and inclination, and aid them in achieving it. They are open parents whose vision is not clouded by wrong beliefs. They do not have rigid 'rules'. But they are disciplined and they teach discipline to their children as well. They establish a communication platform with their children. Hence, the child understands them. They communicate with the child as well as with their friends and teachers. They give praise or punishment at the right time, as required.

They know that if they want their child to bloom like a beautiful flower, they will have to play the role of a good caretaker. They will have to ensure that the flower bed in which they grow is fertile, i.e. the environment at home is happy and conducive. The top soil and mulch that enables the plant to grow well is of highest quality, i.e. the living conditions for the children are the best they can provide. There is trust, confidence, and healthy communication amongst all members of the family. The flower bed must be periodically treated with weed killers so that the plants stay protected. In other words, they protect the children from bad company and unethical behavior. Finally, they provide adequate water and sunlight which are essential for holistic and maximum growth, i.e. the children are provided with good education and good values for them to become good citizens and leaders.

Complete parents demonstrate what they want the child to develop, rather than just preach. They are an example and a role model for their kids. Every parent must be trained in order for their child to be trained. An untrained parent cannot train a child.

From the above six types of parents, the sixth type of 'Bright parents' or 'Complete parents' are the ones who have the right knowledge of parenting. You too can aspire to be a Bright parent by always remembering the following ten points that Bright parents understand and demonstrate.

1) They love their child completely but are not only child-centered. They are complete by themselves too.

2) They do not think of their child as their property. The child is not a means for them to show ownership and authority. They are very clear about this.

3) These parents know that the child has come into this world through them; they do not own the child. Children are God's property and not the means to fulfill their own desires.

4) They communicate well with the child. They answer every question of the child.

5) Such parents do not create obstacles in the path of their children's progress but always help them in their physical, mental, economic, social, and total development.

6) These parents make children understand what to do and what not to do. They awaken their discriminative intelligence *(viveka),* due to which children get inspired to try new experiments. They forgive their mistakes knowing that children learn from their mistakes.

7) Most importantly, they never compare their children with

others, nor do they ever demean them. They bring about a transformation in children through their own behavior.

8) They ask their children questions related to studies to know how much they have progressed in their studies.

9) They intermittently check with whom their children are hanging out with. They chat with their kids' friends, which enables them to know their nature and disposition. They also become friendly with them, which helps them to gain information about any vices or habits their kids or their friends may have developed. If their kids have developed some bad habits due to bad company, they try to slowly change their company.

10) They ensure that their child always keeps good company, because that is crucial for their progress.

The goal of self-development is to become a child again,
to become good and true.
To become true means
realizing your true divine self and living as one.

7
UNDERSTAND YOUR CHILD'S DEFINITION OF LOVE
Read your child's dictionary

Every child needs love and attention from their parents.
If they get the desired love and attention
then they become exactly what their parents want them to be.

Every child has their own dictionary. Every word means differently to every child. Thus, the definition of love is also different for each one of them.

The definition of "love" for parents may not be the same as for their kid. Hence, it is essential for parents to understand their kid's dictionary. Given below are some of the types of love that children need. This will help you understand specifically what your child wants, so that they feel loved, and can thereby grow and progress to the highest extent possible.

1) **Children that need touch**

    Some children want their parents to touch them lovingly and hug them frequently. There are some parents who love their children but don't have the habit of touching them often. In this case, the kids feel they are not loved. When parents cuddle them and snuggle them, they feel loved. Thus, these children's love bank is filled by touch. If this is case with your child, then nurture them with your loving touch.

2) **Children that need praise**

Some kids are okay with not being cuddled but they need to hear some words of praise. If they do something good, they yearn for appreciation. When parents tell them, "I am proud of you," they feel fulfilled. If they are complemented for a drawing they made, it is enough for them. This fills their love bank. You too can look for opportunities to admire and applaud for your kid.

3) **Children that need gifts**

Some children need gifts to feel loved. They don't want words but presents. It does not matter whether the gift is big or small, expensive or cheap. They feel happy just in receiving them. It could be a little flower, a handmade greeting card, or a regular pencil box. They want their parents to bring them something every time in order to believe they are loved. They consider gifts as the evidence of love. If they get hugs and praises but not presents, they feel nobody loves them.

4) **Children that need attention**

Some children want their parents to help them in whatever they do. If they are cutting a piece of paper for craftwork, then they want their parents too to participate with a pair of scissors. This makes them feel loved. They want someone to always tell them whether they are on the right path or not. Such kids are eager to work and learn new skills. They are even ready to work for a long duration but only if they get their parents' attention.

5) **Children that need time**

Some kids want their parents' time and they say, "Don't do anything else for me but be with me." They only need their presence. The presence of their parents is enough for them. It pleases them and nourishes them. Quality time from parents can help such kids to achieve their full potential.

6) Children that need direct words

Some children desire that their parents should tell them in plain words: "I love you so much." They like to hear direct expressions of love. Just listening to these words, they become ready to work a lot. Since they are tuned with words, they also feel very happy when their parents bring them a book or knowledge in any form.

As a parent, we have to fill the love bank of our kids based on their definition of love, which will inspire them to achieve their goals. Some children need to be shown that they are loved in two or more ways. For example, a child may desire time as well as gifts from parents. It is not necessary that a kid should desire love in only one way. There can be all kinds of kids. We need to express our love to our children regularly according to their requirement. Otherwise, some parents love their children very much but are unable to express it in the desired manner, due to which the kids feel they are neither understood nor loved. That is why it is critical to know what will fill the love bank of your child.

Out of the six types described above, try to find your child's requirement and then express your love accordingly.

Parents are the first teachers of a child,
while teachers are their second parents.
Children can become teachers of their parents
and true disciples of their teachers.

8
QUALITIES REQUIRED IN PARENTS
Balancing Love and Discipline

Right appreciation in the right measure at the right time,
and if a mistake is committed, then right punishment
in the right measure at the right time,
is essential for the progress of a child.

If you were given a chance to choose your parents again, then what kind of parents would you choose? What attributes would you want them to possess?

Out of all the attributes that you would desire in your parents, three are presented below. After considering all three, you can decide which ones you would like to see in your parents.

1) **Money**

   Ask yourself if you want your parents to be rich. Honestly ask yourself if you really need wealthy parents.

2) **Understanding**

   Do you want your parents to have the quality of understanding? Such kind of parents know what their children want; they understand their needs. They have the knowledge to understand things. So, do you want these kind of parents?

3) Time

Some parents have a lot of money but no time for their children. Such kids would most probably choose parents who can give them time.

Different kids will desire different attributes in their parents. Some will feel money is more important, while some understanding. As mentioned, children who don't get time from their parents will wish for parents who can do so. Kids whose parents cannot give them money will desire rich parents who can buy them gifts and everything else they want. There will be some children who feel it's important for their parents to have the knowledge of understanding.

Some parents have money but not the time or knowledge. Some parents have knowledge but neither time nor money. Some children say it's fine if their parents don't have anything else, they just want their parents to spend time with them.

However, if parents have all these three attributes, then their children can really blossom to achieve their maximum potential. It is not possible for all parents to have all three attributes. Some would have one of these, while some may have two. There can be ones who have all three.

Below are given three options, each with a pair of attributes:

1. Knowledge and money
2. Knowledge and time
3. Time and money

If children are asked to choose only one of the above combinations for their parents, which will they choose?

Some would choose money and time, but most would choose

knowledge and money or knowledge and time. That's because most people are aware that with knowledge and time, money can be earned. One would choose attributes based on all that one has gone through. If you are a parent, then deeply reflect on which of these elements are the most important for the development of your child. And those are the ones that you will need to cultivate.

Importance of discipline in parents

Let's say if one more attribute were to be added which could enhance all the other three elements, what would it be? It's discipline. If parents have discipline, then they can reap the benefits of all the other attributes in abundance.

Undisciplined parents may be ready to give time to their kids, but are entangled so much in their own problems. They are untrained and that's why they keep things somewhere and forget, then they cannot find anything nor complete their work on time. The time of such parents is not helpful to their children. Unfortunately, if parents are undisciplined, then their kids too fail to develop discipline. What the children see is what they learn.

If parents are disciplined and trained, then what will the life of their kids be like? What kind of revolution would these kids bring on growing up? Such children understand the goal of life right from their childhood. The kids of undisciplined parents grow up without any aim. They can earn money but they don't do anything for the society. On the other hand, if parents possess discipline in addition to time, money, and knowledge, then their children become capable of heralding a great revolution in this world.

Significance of giving and forgiving

If parents follow a true spiritual master and have imbibed the master's teachings, then based on those teachings they are able to impart the highest and best knowledge and training to their children. A child who has received training, discipline, and wisdom can perform great miracles in the world.

When a true guru comes into your life and you attain wisdom, then you understand the significance of giving. If you are unable to forgive the mistakes of your children, then they grow up with a sense of guilt. Hence, forgiving is a critical quality in parents for proper development of their children. Also, if you are able to give unconditionally to your children, then later on they too would do the same for others. This is an important life lesson for them.

If kids feel their parents never gave them unconditionally nor forgave their mistakes, then they too are unable to forgive others easily. If parents beat their kids, then those kids most often do the same with their own children. The daughter-in-law who was abused by her mother-in-law, what kind of mother-in-law would she become later on? She will most probably abuse her daughter-in-law too. In this way, the vicious cycle continues.

Punishment and Praise

Fully knowing and understanding their kids, with the best intentions in mind, parents have to take the right decision to punish or praise their kids as required at a given time. If parents are able to do this at the right time and with good intentions, then gradually there remains no need for punishment. Often parents make the mistake of not giving the right appreciation or punishment to their kid at the right time and in the right measure.

Punish your kid at the right time

When a child makes a mistake for the first time and is punished at that very time in the right amount, then the need for a bigger punishment in the future does not arise. A few words uttered by the parents at the right time could be a big punishment for a child.

Punishing at the right time means taking action when an incident occurs for the first time. Suppose, your kid stole something for the first time and you reprimanded and expressed your disappointment in adequate words, or gave some other suitable punishment. If nothing is done at that time, then the kid could possibly indulge in bigger crimes and become a criminal in the future. Crime could become their pattern or tendency, which is then difficult to break.

Therefore, punishment at the right time is essential. After growing up, such kids often thank their parents. "It's good that you stopped me at the right time, and helped break those bad habits in time. You also taught me the importance of saving money at the right time. Otherwise, I would never be able to save, and all my life I would be running behind money. Now I understand the secrets that you told me about life and its various aspects, which is helping me to grow internally and externally. So, thank you for the punishment at that time."

There are some parents who punish their kids very often. Subsequently, these kids lose their sensitivity toward it, and the disciplining fails to yield any good results that the parents were expecting. If the right punishment is not given at the right time and in the right amount, then it becomes necessary to give a bigger punishment in the future, but by then the child has already become desensitized to it. The child thinks this is how adults are; they always keep shouting and punishing. In this way, constant punishment desensitizes the kids and then the parents keep on complaining why their kids are not improving. If you want to improve your kids, then you need to bring some changes in yourself first. You need to get trained in how to train your kids.

Praise your kid at the right time

The same principle applies to praise as well. If you appreciate your kids at the right time and using the right words, you will find that they blossom quickly and explore their highest potential.

When you watch a cricket match, and if the batsman hits a four, you can see that the spectators clap for him at once, not after ten minutes. If they clap after the time has passed, the batsman wouldn't know why they are clapping. The same is the case with kids. If they do something good, it is essential to appreciate them right away. If we don't pay attention to them at that time, they feel disappointed, and then after some days if we tell them they did good *that* day, it has lost its importance. Hence, it is necessary for everything to happen at the right time.

If parents have discipline,
they can reap the benefit of their other attributes
in abundance.

9
HOW DO CHILDREN LEARN?
You are the rode model of your kids

*When a child learns to walk, it stumbles and falls many times
but then gets up again. We ought to learn from the child.
Every stumble should teach us something.
We have to rise after every fall;
and not empty-handed but with a lesson.*

Children spend six to seven hours at school but the place where they spend most of their time is at home. Young children have a keen sense of observation. They learn a lot by observing things around them. How do mom and dad talk to each other? How do they get angry on one another? What words do they use? A kid listens and watches everything carefully and then imitates their behavior. Hence, every parent needs to keep in mind how they behave in front of their kids and what words they use. The young child may not know the meaning of your words but believes that if mom or dad has said something then it must be good. So, later on when this kid suddenly repeats the same words in the presence of guests or openly in the house, then parents find themselves in an embarrassing situation or feel upset about it.

Children learn some things by listening to the people in the society they live in. They learn a lot from TV, radio, and internet. That is why, it is important for parents to check what their kid is watching and listening. The child may learn some good things from a few television programs, but most programs inspire them to live in a fantasy.

A child picks up and emulates whatever the relatives, neighbors, and teachers do. If parents lie frequently, then the child learns to do the same. Thus, they unknowingly train their kid to lie. No parent wants this. But by watching them, the child quickly learns how to lie and get things done.

> For instance, a man sees a guest approaching their house, and in order to avoid that guest, he instructs his son, "When that uncle rings the bell, you should open the door and tell him that I am not at home." The guest rings the bell and the little boy opens the door. The guest says, "Hello, young man! Is your father at home?" The boy instantly replies, "My father has told me to tell you that he's not at home."

Children are free from deceit, falsity, and hypocrisy; they are honest, true, and innocent. Hence, we have to always watch out whether our actions are creating bad habits in our kids.

Some kids absorb a lot by reading books. If that's the case, then it becomes the duty of the parents to bring them those books which will teach them something good, so that they can progress and achieve their goals.

All children learn from what they experience. The house in which they live and its atmosphere, the school in which they study and every little thing in it leaves a deep impression upon a child.

Some kids learn mostly from people. How people behave with them is how they end up behaving with people when they grow up. This is why every parent needs to keep in mind that their behavior with their kids should be how they want their kids to behave with them.

Most children learn through curiosity. Be it a little kid or an older one, they always want to experiment. They observe every little thing that goes on in their surroundings with curious eyes. They want to understand every incident and every little thing from different angles. Such children have the potential to become inventors. In this case, parents will have to help their children enhance their abilities and continue to encourage them.

Whatever kids see and hear during their childhood leaves a lasting impression on them and actually shapes them. When they grow up and want to do something, they draw inspiration from the lessons and knowledge they gained as a child. If they are not given due attention during their formative years, then the inventor in them dies.

Every parent should attempt to become a role model for their child. They have to always ask themselves: "What image are we presenting to our kids? What do our children think of us? What do they believe us to be?" Every parent needs to work on this aspect.

> A father and his son used to pray together at night every day. One day, the father asked his son, "What did you pray today?" The boy earnestly replied, "I prayed to God to make me just like my dad when I grow up." The man was stunned. His prayer changed from that day. He started praying, "Dear God, please make me exactly as my son sees me and thinks of me."

All parents need to create an environment at home that portrays their image in a way which is inspiring and motivating for their kids.

In order to develop your children,
you need to work on your intention.
Have a clear intention behind every step you take.

*Whatever you are doing for your kids
in the present,
do it in the best manner.
Whatever you did for them in the past,
learn your lessons from it and forget it.
Whatever you will do for them tomorrow,
have faith that it will be great.*

Nine Positive Steps

1. Boost your child's self-confidence
2. Encourage them and give them unconditional love
3. Understand what upsets them through good communication
4. Understand their merits and demerits
5. Teach them using play and games
6. Take care of their health
7. Recognize their potential
8. Teach them the importance of failure
9. Strengthen their character

10
GIVE THE RIGHT TRAINING TO YOUR KIDS
How to develop self-confidence in children

*If there is friendship and good communication
between parents and kids,
then soon these kids will grow and create
a highly evolved world and work for their growth.*

How should children be trained? What is the best method to train them? How to effectively cultivate positive habits in children? The answer to all of these questions can be beautifully illustrated by the following example that describes how a dolphin is trained. Let's take a look at it.

Suppose the goal is to teach a dolphin to jump across a rope tied high above the pool surface.

So, at the beginning of this training, a rope is tied quite low under the surface of water. When the dolphin is swimming about in the water, it is watched throughout the day. During this leisure swimming, whenever it swims above the rope, a piece of food is thrown to it at once. This is done every single time. Whenever it crosses over the rope, it gets food and not otherwise. Slowly, the dolphin begins to understand that there is a definite relation between swimming above the rope and getting food. Therefore, it starts crossing over the rope repeatedly and every time it is rewarded with food.

Gradually, the rope is tied a little higher inside the water, and the same training method is repeated. As the dolphin adapts to it, the rope is tied even more higher under the water. This procedure continues progressively until the rope touches the surface of the water. With the rope at the surface, the dolphin cannot just swim across it. If it wants food, it will now have to come out of the water. Only when it jumps in the air over the rope, it's rewarded. Then a whistle is blown every time it jumps. Eventually, the whistle, the food, and the jumping over the rope get linked with each other inside the dolphin's cognitive system. During further training, the rope is tied high in the air, well above the water surface. The dolphin can jump across it too. Going ahead, even the rope is taken away. Now it jumps just on hearing the whistle.

This is how a dolphin is trained in a step-by-step manner. When these dolphins display astonishing feats during a show, people are amazed thinking how these fish must have been trained and what could be its secret! They wonder how a fish can understand when to jump and when to dive and how to perform so many amazing tricks accurately. It looks simply miraculous. However, the fact is that the trainers have put in a lot of time, love, and effort. They have the information and knowledge about dolphins, about how they operate, when they need attention, and when they don't need the rope. They observe and pay a lot of attention to the dolphins.

Parents too need to constantly pay attention to their kids. They will have to be aware of when a child needs what. They have to check from time to time what their children are thinking, to what extent are they interested in studies, sports, or other activities, and what kind of friends they have. Just as a dolphin is constantly watched, parents too need to always keep an eye over their child. As children grow, you have to give them the necessary training, a new way of thinking, and new information, at every step. You have to develop their scientific knowledge. Just as a dolphin is trained progressively by raising the rope, likewise a young child can be trained starting with baby steps all the way up to complete training.

When your children become fully trained, then there is no need to keep them tied down. They understand on their own. A fish doesn't know what it needs to do, but a human child knows what to do and when because they have a brain. They can think. They can choose a goal for themselves. Although, initially, they don't know what is good and what is bad for them. They are not aware how harmful wrong tendencies, bad habits, vices, and addictions can be for them.

An uneducated child initially likes a life of bad habits and addictions. If they listen to you, then have a serious talk with them. If they don't, then find out who they like to be with and who do they listen to. If your child listens to his teacher, then you can meet the teacher and make a request. "My kid has this habit, so while teaching if you can please say something about this habit, he will understand." This can really help the kids to get rid of their bad habits and cultivate good ones. The purpose of parents-teachers meeting in every school is to allow exchange of information about the kids between the two parties. This helps in giving the right guidance to the child both at home and at school.

With the right guidance and counseling, the child will realize, "These habits of mine are the biggest obstacle in achieving my goals. Half my life will be gone in forming these habits and the other half in eradicating them!" On realizing this fact, they are shaken up and then they begin to fully participate in the training for their growth being imparted by their parents.

While training their children, parents have to keep in mind the following three crucial points:

1) Make your child a master in one field

If you want to bolster the self-confidence of your child, then help them gain mastery in one particular field. It does not matter even if it's a small field. When a child is able to do something better than the others, they start feeling confident.

Can your child sing better than others? Can your child draw better than others? Can your child write better poetry? Can your child run faster? Can your child cook better? Can your child be the life of a party? Can your child play better piano or guitar? Can your child narrate stories better? Is your child's handwriting better than others? Any of these skills may or may not appear to be something major, but on developing excellence in a certain skill, your child will gain immense self-confidence. Hence, all parents should help their kids to excel in at least one skill. This will spur them to achieve excellence in other subjects at school too.

Before a child can achieve mastery in any field, you have to mentally prepare them. First, you have to decide whether the task your child is going to perform is possible for them. In other words, are they capable of performing those tasks that an average person can? Some of those tasks may be a bit difficult or your child may initially feel that way, but you have to encourage them and convince them that they can do it and they should do it. Explain to them, "If one person in the world can do it, so can you. And if millions of people can do it, then you most definitely can."

Mastery in a particular field is a boon for a child. One child could be an expert in drawing while the other could be unbeatable in math. In whatever subject your child is interested, you can motivate them to top in that subject. Don't push your child to top every subject. All parents want their kids to be toppers. But as you know it is not possible for all the kids to top the class. However, what your child can certainly do is to excel in one particular subject. You have to be aware which subject that could be. It could be a subject of his studies or it could be something else. It could be a sport, an indoor game, outdoor game, a scientific game, computers, music, dance, painting, poetry, doodling, history, geography, or anything else.

Just tell your child, "Be an expert in one subject." It is necessary to study all the subjects to pass in exams but find out the subject or activity for which your child has an interest, an inclination, the aptitude and qualities for excelling. Motivate them for that subject, make them work hard on that subject, and make them feel there is no one better than them in that subject. This confidence will work wonders for them.

Enhancing the self-confidence of the child is an invaluable gift from the parents, which proves to be a blessing throughout their lives. Every parent can give this gift to their children so that these kids are filled with confidence and have a good self-image. Such children would be totally confident that they can do anything because they have already achieved success in one field and are already ahead in it.

2) **Say positive words for your kids**

When guests visit your home, you should say positive words to your kids in front of them. This increases their self-confidence. If you tell your child, "Don't pick up that glass, you will drop it," this will reduce their confidence. Do not commit the mistake of not allowing your kid to handle the glass because it may break. Remember that even if they shatter one expensive glass, it's okay, but the confidence that they will feel by holding that glass on their own is far more precious. Don't crush your child's confidence. If by mistake, they happen to drop the glass, avoid pouncing on them right away. "See, I told you that you'll break the glass, you cannot do it, you won't be able to do it..." Such words will kill their confidence.

After this incident, the kid will depend on the parents for doing every little thing. They will feel they cannot do anything and that the parents will shout at them whenever they do something. Their hands may shake while doing anything and they may always feel scared inside, which can be very damaging for them.

Some parents always rebuke their child, and the child always remembers those rebukes. This causes the confidence of the child to crash in childhood itself. Such parents need to develop the habit of speaking properly with their kids.

Words have great power. They can build your child or break them. Therefore, always use positive words for them and with them.

3) Develop your child's self-esteem

Parents need to develop a healthy self-esteem in their kids. This will increase their self-confidence. On attaining this confidence, they will be successful in whatever they undertake. Provide a platform for your kid just like a film director.

In order to do so, you can give your kid the responsibility to plan and organize a small event. If there is a birthday in the family, you can tell your kid, "Your brother's birthday is going to be celebrated on this date. You are responsible for this event. You have to fully plan and organize it. You decide how many people will be invited, how much money should be spent, and what all items would be required. Create a list and timetable for these activities and then carry them out. We will only guide you in the process but it's you who has to do it."

Listening to this, the kid may initially hesitate and say they don't know all these things. But you can convince them. "You *can* do this and you have to do it." When the child starts organizing the event, then with every event, their confidence will rise. You can inform them of your budget and deadline, and tell them to do the rest. When they successfully organize the event in the given budget and time period (with or without any flaws), their confidence will increase and they will develop a healthy self-esteem. In this way, allow your kids to experiment.

If you really want your kid to become totally ready
before they step into the world,
then you will have to develop them like a super hit film.
Then, when they are released (or step) into the world,
people would be amazed and left wondering
how one individual can have so many qualities!

11
GIVE UNCONDITIONAL LOVE
Raise your child's morale

We don't have to focus on how our kids are wrong,
but how they are right.
We have to awaken the Divine residing in them.

Many parents discriminate between their children. If there is a son and a daughter, or a younger and older son in the family, they treat them differently. Some parents feel that their son will be their support in their old age, while their daughter will get married and go and live with her new family. Therefore, they treat their children on the basis of such thinking. Between two sons, if the younger is good in studies and the older is not so good, then they constantly compare the two. They criticize the older son in front of the younger and humiliate him. This gives rise to a feeling of hatred in the older child.

There are some parents who keep on scolding their children or even hit them for their mistakes, but it has been seen that this does not bring about an improvement. If a child makes a mistake, such parents always say, "*You* have done this, you are *wrong*, you don't *understand* anything." Never tell the child that he or she is wrong, instead tell them what they have done wrong. A child does not make blunders deliberately. When they understand their mistake, they want to know how to rectify it. If you get things done by reprimanding and punishing, it teaches your kids that this is the only way to get things done. Sometimes, some parents vent their anger by hitting their children. This creates fear or a feeling of vengeance in the children. When the child fails in an exam, some parents get very angry and express their anger upon the child. This makes the child feel insecure.

If you want to raise their morale, then motivate them. Always use positive words with them. Tell them lovingly, "You have not failed; you just haven't attained success yet." Such words will reduce your child's despair. "Even if you fail, our love for you will never diminish." These words open new doors of success for your kids and fill them with self-confidence. Never attach labels to your child like, "You have *failed*. Now you'll never be able to do anything. You are an idiot and a fool." Such words create an inferiority complex in the child. Laughing at the mistakes of your kid damages their self-esteem. If you want to become ideal parents for your children, then never behave negatively with them.

On the other hand, many parents take excessive care of their kids even after they are grown up. The kid may be going to college, still they keep bombarding them with instructions and endless questions. "Sit like this… Why did you do this?… Where have you been?… What are you doing?" If you want your children to improve their decision-making skills, then allow them to take their own decisions. You can give your suggestions and recommendations, but leave the decision to them. This will develop their self-confidence and the habit of making decisions. If you want your kid to cultivate certain qualities, then your unconditional love and making them feel independent will help in this endeavor.

Some parents unintentionally create a wrong habit in their kids by putting up conditions: "If you score these many marks in your exam,

I'll buy you your favorite toy." If you want to motivate your child or make them achieve their goal, it's not a good idea to place conditions on them. Children want their parents to love them unconditionally. Hence, it is said that your presence and attitude rather than your presents have a greater impact on your child. When children realize that their mom and dad love them no matter what and will always support them, then they too will begin to love and cooperate with you unconditionally.

When children become capable of taking up some responsibility, give them adequate freedom. When they are a bit grown up, talk to them about the household matters or about your business, and ask their opinion. Never think that consulting your children is a sign of weakness. The day the child starts feeling that you only want their well-being, they will also start talking openly with you. There is one place at home where you can talk freely with your kids, and that is the dining table. When all the family members have dinner together, the bond between them becomes stronger. The food that parents and children eat together not only makes their bodies healthy but also their relationship.

*If there are children in your house,
then you have received an opportunity
to once again become a child.*

12
THE MANTRA FOR A HAPPY FAMILY: GOOD COMMUNICATION

Understand your child's displeasure

Never let the blessings we have received
turn into a curse because of our unawareness.
The little bundle of joy that has arrived in our family is a blessing.
It has come to teach us to become a child again.
By spoiling them, don't let them turn into a curse.

All parents feel they should do something for their children. A child is a cherished dream of the parents. You desire to provide the best education to your children and are ready to do anything to make that happen. You want your family to always be happy. But are you taking the right steps in that direction? With this question, some other questions also come to the fore, such as:

1) Do you always talk with your children? Do you give them enough time?

2) What do you consider your children to be while interacting with them?

3) Do you speak to your kids with respect?

4) When your child does not listen to you, do you try to find the reason behind it?

5) Do your kids share everything that happens in their life with you?

6) Do you treat all your children equally?

7) Do you pay attention to changes that occur in your children?

8) Do you become an inspiration for your kids?

When many such queries arise, then some things definitely come to light. If every parent asks themselves these questions, they will find all the answers within them.

Good Communication with Children

We feel that if we are sending our children to a good school and giving them whatever they want, our work is done. Now they should study well and achieve something big. They should fulfill all our expectations and aspirations.

When this does not happen, a rift begins to form in our relationship with them. We feel our kid should become a doctor, engineer, or lawyer. There is nothing wrong with this expectation. But are we aware of the intellectual capacity of our child? Our child may excel in a different area because that is their disposition, a part of their constitution. But we want our child to become what we desire. This is a mistake made by many parents. We never ponder over what our child has come to express in this world. Do we inspire them for that self-expression? Instead, we always think that our child is our property and we have full rights over them. With this belief, we try to make them as we desire. Is this right?

Due to this belief, we feel that our child should do whatever we want and we always talk to them on that basis. Is this good communication with our children? When the child makes a mistake, instead of making them understand, we scold them and make taunting remarks. We also repeatedly flaunt our experiences to make them feel bad. "When I was your age, this is what I used to do…" Do narrate your experiences to your kids but don't give them the impression of: "I was right and see how wrongly you are doing this." Always remember that our child is not the means to fulfill our desires. They are not an object that we can own. They are a free life which took birth in our family. They are free individuals and have full right to live freely. Thereby, we should try our best to provide them the environment that is conducive to the kind of self-expression our child is born with. We should pay attention to find out what they like and encourage them to communicate their interests and inclination. When we come to know which subject or field our child is interested in, what their disposition is suited for, then it is our duty to develop them accordingly. Children who are brought up in this manner will certainly open up, blossom, and achieve success in life.

> There was an ordinary boy in school, who was not at all good in his studies. The school teachers told the parents, "He will never progress. He is addled (stupid) and has no interest in the subjects being taught at school." Some years later, this very boy went on to make hundreds of discoveries and inventions. This boy was Thomas Edison.

It is often seen that many parents compare their child with other children, and say, "The neighbor's son is so good in studies. He is going to become a doctor. You don't study at all. You have no interest in studies. He will progress in life and you will remain behind…" At such times, parents forget that such words create guilt and a feeling of inferiority in the child. The child becomes jealous of others. Therefore, never allow this demon of comparison to enter your child. Always consider and take care of your child's feelings.

Always remember that when we do something for the development of the child, it should not be through wrong means. You can inform your child about your financial situation. Giving the child everything but through wrong means is spoiling the child, because children learn a lot by observing the behavior of their parents. Hence, whenever a child does something wrong, every parent should carry out a self-introspection. Children behave according to what they see or hear at home and that is what seeps into their life.

Communication without getting emotional

It is a great training for children to see you communicate without getting emotional throughout the day. Thus, it is important to pay attention to your emotions and keep control before saying anything in front of your child.

A child comes home happily from school and starts narrating what happened in school. "Mom, you know what happened today… one boy did this… one girl did that… then I did this…" Mom starts shouting at once. "Then why didn't you say this… you should have done that…" The child is taken aback. "What happened suddenly to mom? Why is she getting so emotional?" From then on, they feel uncertain. "If I say this, I don't know how they will react. Will they shout and scream at me?" Due to this fear, they eventually stop sharing anything at home. Gradually, they become closed in their life.

In contrast, suppose you had reacted calmly. "Honey, now that you were there, this is what you could have said… or this is what you could have done… But it's fine; don't worry about it. You can just remember this for the next time." Listening to your response, the child realizes the truth. This happened because they paid attention only to your calm and straight words.

Thus, it is important to use neutral language when your child shares any occurrence with you. Avoid expressing through your emotions or actions that something bad has happened with them or they have done something bad. The child learns from such conversations and doesn't feel scared of you. If you can talk to your kid normally without getting carried away, then your kid would share everything with you. If something happens with them, they would like to come and tell you about it. They would feel better and lighter after sharing with you.

Otherwise, hearing you shout that they should have done this or done that, they get scared and wonder how to tell you the truth or whether to tell you anything at all. Children don't realize how harmful it can prove to be when they don't tell you anything. At that time, they are only concerned about escaping your scolding, punishment, or what you express through your emotions. So, they lie or don't tell you anything at all.

There is this instance of a boy who had shared at home an incident that had occurred with a classmate. After that, he was troubled so much by his parents even though the event did not involve him at all. All he had done was to share it with them. He was questioned and lectured so much about it, that from then on from his school to his college days he never shared anything with his family. This was a great loss. The second loss was that he could not say anything openly to anyone in his life. It had become a habit for him to suppress everything within himself. Later, when he joined Tej Gyan Foundation, he was suggested to write his experiences, which enabled him to experience freedom. Only then he began to open up.

There are so many children who remain suppressed. They are unable to open up in front of anyone. This is very harmful for them. Some people who are aware of this situation may take advantage of them because they know they can do anything to them and these kids will not share it with their elders. How dangerous is this! Hence, parents, teachers, and other elders should think how they should behave in front of children.

If your parents used to react harshly, which caused you to close down, it is highly unfortunate, and you would not want to pass this to your next generation. Therefore, you will have to learn to express your feelings and thoughts calmly. Even if you are very angry or anger is arising in you, yet if you are able to communicate calmly that you felt bad or you did not like something, it will be a great help, a wonderful lesson, and a valuable gift to your child.

Always give your child an opportunity to share what they want to. It's possible that they are initially unable to express properly because they don't yet possess communication skills and neither have they taken a course in communication, but your simple and neutral responses will teach them how to converse with you.

Bad communication is better than no communication

While dealing with children, remember that bad communication by them is always better than no communication. When children express their displeasure and break stuff, you get angry. You feel, why are they doing this? Actually, they want to convey to you that they are upset. Children are not aware of better ways of expressing their unhappiness, so they act out. Adults get upset too but they express it in such a way that nobody feels they are doing something wrong. This is because adults have become trained to hide their negative feelings and express them in different ways. Children are not aware of any such methods, so they do what they feel like.

If children do anything to express their unhappiness, parents should actually be happy because the kids are trying to communicate with them. Only they don't know any better method to do it, hence it is the responsibility of parents to explain to the child. "You could have expressed your feelings in a different way. There are better ways to express discontent, dislike, and anger. If you use this particular method to express your displeasure, your desire will be fulfilled sooner. If you break something, it will delay the fulfillment of your desire."

When you explain it to the kids, they understand. They realize that if they had acted differently, daddy would have agreed at once, but since they expressed it harshly, it took some time. Slowly, they will understand this fact and then begin to express and articulate their feelings in a better manner. It is the duty of parents to teach better ways of communication to their children so that they can express their feelings, and that too without hurting anyone.

In ignorance, children may commit some mistakes during childhood that has a long-term impact. Those mistakes could be stealing, lying, avoiding work, or doing something which is prohibited. Most of the times, parents just cannot understand why are their kids doing this? What is happening with them at school or in the neighborhood, that they are comparing themselves with other kids? What is diminishing their self-confidence? From where are they learning these things?

If a communication platform has been established between parents and children, then parents can get this information from their kids and understand all these issues. They can then provide the right guidance at the right time, and the problem could be nipped in the bud. Otherwise, later on, these kids and everyone else in the family will have to suffer the consequences of their bad habits. Parents are the biggest well-wishers of their children, hence it is their first duty to remove everything that is bad in their kids and bring them on the path of good.

How to live life? How to look at every event with a positive outlook? How to accept the problems that appear in life and how to find the solutions? You have to teach and communicate all of this in the best manner to your kids. Don't let your negative experiences or compulsions made on you by your parents during your childhood affect your children. Allow your kids to live their lives according to their natural inherent qualities, so that when they grow up they can choose a path that will allow them their highest self-expression.

13

OPEN UP, BLOSSOM, AND PLAY WITH CHILDREN

Teach children through play

The meaning of progress is to attain physical, mental, emotional, social, financial, and spiritual maturity. Therefore, strive for complete progress of your children.

Every human being needs to progress in all five major aspects of life—physical, mental, social, financial, and spiritual. Complete parents develop their child in all these areas, so that the child achieves total development.

For social development, parents take care to ensure that their children get such environment and are surrounded by such people that they can develop socially. This setting helps children to understand relationships and share each other's joys and sorrows.

Children begin to develop well on a mental level when they get inspiration, security, and love from their parents. Good communication between parents and kids enhances their mental development.

Children begin to learn about the financial aspect as they start growing up. If they develop the habit of saving and not spending unnecessarily, and are able to understand the difference between needs and wants right from childhood, then they can progress very well in the financial aspect on growing up.

When kids are 18-19 years of age, they begin to understand higher things, and this is the time they can develop their spiritual side, which is a very important part of life. If they get this most crucial understanding of "What is the ultimate purpose of my life?", they grow spiritually. On growing spiritually, they become "Bright" householders and later on Bright parents. Bright householders are neither monks nor attached to the material world. They live in the world and with the spiritual wisdom they have acquired, they lead a life filled with understanding and happiness.

For physical development, we need to know and teach our children: How to keep the body healthy? What kind of foods and drinks will keep it fit and strong? And what should be avoided to prevent harming the body? The other four aspects of life can be easily developed if our body is healthy. It is all the more essential to take care of the health of a child because the foundation of physical ability is laid in childhood itself.

The question that arises therefore is what should be done in their early years to take steps toward complete development? The answer lies in play and games.

Importance of playing

When children are 2–3 years old, ensure that they start playing such games which will increase their physical, mental, and intellectual ability. Giving them expensive toys is not a solution; you have to teach them to go out and play on the ground, and enjoy themselves in the open air.

However, nowadays it is often seen that instead of playing outside in the evening, little children sit and watch cartoons, action movies, and other shows on TV. They pick up many wrong habits from these programs. They may become stubborn, prefer to remain alone, and may also indulge in violence. Before such symptoms start developing in our kids, we need to become aware and alert. We certainly have to keep an eye on which programs they watch.

As soon as a child is born from the mother's womb, it begins to learn something or the other. (In fact, they learn a lot while in the womb too.) As children begin to grow, they love to play various games. These games are very beneficial for their development. First of all, they learn, "How to play this game?" If a certain game requires concentration, they put in efforts to develop concentration. If a game requires intelligence, they work on it too, so as to become an expert in that game. They learn to work hard. They know that if they want to become a champion in a game, they have to be dedicated and play better than all the others. Children develop all these qualities while playing games.

When a young child picks up some object and starts playing with it, observe them carefully. They turn that object and look at it from every angle, they bang it repeatedly against some surface to see what sound it makes and what happens to it. Everything feels new to a child, everything seems a miracle. And this is how they begin to learn about the world around them. The questions they ask may seem strange but are very important. If we pay attention to those questions, we will realize how imaginative, inquisitive, and aware these little ones are.

"Why is the ball round?" "Why does a train run only on rails?" "How many stars are there in the sky?" "Why can't we see the moon during the day?" "Why only children have to go to school?" There are many such questions that young children ask their parents. Your child too may have asked you. So, how do most parents answer these questions? If they don't have the answers to some questions, they avoid them or scold the child. "Don't ask such foolish questions."

However, if we think about it, we will realize that the child's language, thinking, and research ability develops through this questioning. These questions show their curiosity and their need to know things. They grow by inquiring and seeing and learning new things. Hence, whenever children present such queries or request you to play some unusual game with them, oblige them. Try to answer them and play with them because these very queries and games augment their zeal, spirit of inquiry, confidence, and patience. The first companions to play with children are their parents.

Whatever games your kids like to play, you can teach them a lot through games. You can reveal new things to them. You can show them other possibilities in that game. Hence, don't regard it as nonsense, and play with them as often as possible. If you let them play what they want to and let them do what they need to do in the game, they learn more quickly. When the kid works hard in a game and achieves something, the happiness on their face is something to behold. On growing up a bit, when they go to school and play with friends by forming a group, they learn the importance of teamwork. They learn how to stay together in harmony with each other and what is sportsmanship. Games and sports aid children in imbibing many wonderful qualities, which help them to progress in life.

When small children play, their emotions are attached to the game. Their feelings are expressed beautifully through games. Sometimes, you may have seen that when children are angry, they throw things, bang their toys on the floor, and scream. Whenever a little kid throws a tantrum and is adamant about doing something, it is essential for parents to be patient and self-controlled. The kid is trying and fighting to do something new, something difficult, and may feel frustrated or thrilled in the process. All these are steps in their development.

If there is no risk involved in such games, then let the child play such games. For example, we often find a child stacking building blocks on top of each other. At one stage, all the blocks fall down. He collects all the blocks and again tries to stack them. The blocks collapse once more. After several attempts, the kid gets irritated and scatters the blocks all around. After some time, he collects the blocks and tries again. After a while, he succeeds in stacking 8-10 blocks and begins to laugh and jump with joy. His eyes gleam with confidence and the sense of achievement. Such games teach him: *Never get defeated by defeat.*

If the child requires your help in such games, then try to assist them. Let the child feel that their parents are with them. This feeling helps them to try and to succeed. Along with mental development, their physical development also takes place with these fun and games.

Whenever it is possible and when there is no risk involved, let children take their own decisions. This will increase their decision making ability. Children learn many lessons from success and failure. That is why we have to always encourage and inspire them.

The meaning of progress is to open up and blossom and develop the spirit of sportsmanship.

14
HOW TO BRING ABOUT COMPLETE DEVELOPMENT OF CHILDREN
Virtues and vices of kids

The past cannot be changed
and the present cannot be escaped.
You can only work in the present to brighten the future.
Your kids are the future of this world; make them shine.

Opening up of the complete possibility of the body, mind, and intellect is called complete development. Let's take a look at how it can be achieved in your child.

1) **For development of the body:** Give your children balanced food. As they grow, develop the habits of *pranayam* and exercise in them.

2) **For development of the mind:** Always use positive words with children. Always encourage them. Do not make them feel inferior. Inspire them to decide on a goal and to achieve it.

3) **For development of the intellect:** Teach them practical knowledge and common sense. Let them take their own decisions.

4) **For complete development:** Develop the habit of reading good books in your kids. Buy them self-development books, so that they can read and get inspiration.

Every parent has to be aware for the complete development of their child. Children are like clay. They take whatever shape you give them. If you want to make your child a good human being, then it is important to develop every aspect of their lives. It should be the goal of every parent that the child born in their family should open up, blossom, and express itself in the highest manner. To achieve this, the following steps will be very helpful for every parent.

Step 1 : Without direction, there can be no progress in this world. Learn to give proper direction and proper guidance to your kids.

Step 2 : Make your children capable of achieving their goals. When children grow up and decide their career, they have a goal which they want to attain. Hence, they have to be made capable of achieving their goal. Once they are capable, they will easily achieve it, because one of the principles of life is: *Whatever you become ready for, it will automatically come into your life.*

Step 3 : Develop a sense of responsibility in children. If your child wants to take up some responsibility, don't stop them. Whether the child is young or grown up, when they take up a responsibility and complete it, their eyes light up with confidence. This self-confidence enables them to accept bigger responsibilities in life.

Step 4 : Without positive thinking, no development takes place. When children grow up and want to do some creative work, for which they have an inclination and the disposition, don't try to stop them by using negative words. They need positive inspiration for such work. Make the right use of the power of words to help them attain their goal.

Step 5 : Develop leadership qualities in your child. There are two kinds of people in the world: leaders and followers. You have to develop your kids into leaders. You have to cultivate the qualities of a good leader in them.

Step 6 : Break the thought of failure and limitations of progress. Tell your kids there is no limit to progress. Make them aware that negative thinking, lack of confidence, and wrong beliefs reduce the speed of their progress. Hence, they should avoid words that invite failure, such as, "I can't." Inculcate the feeling of "I can" in your kids.

Step 7 : The word "impossible" does not exist in the dictionary of children. Always teach them to have a strong willpower and firm determination. Remove the word "impossible" from your child's dictionary and replace it with "challenge."

Step 8 : Even huge goals can be attained through some small qualities. Teach children to give up bad habits. If you want complete development of your child, ensure to cultivate certain qualities in them because it is through these small qualities that the ladder of progress can be climbed. Courage, patience, contemplation, honesty, commitment, self-confidence, unwavering faith in God, and fearlessness are virtues that should be imbibed by kids right from their childhood.

Step 9 : If children learn to study a given subject consistently, they are bound to attain success. No goal can be attained without hard work. It is important to begin work and also to continuously work on it. Develop the habit of hard work in your children.

Which qualities should we inculcate in our kids and which habits should be uprooted? Let's refer to the following table.

QUALITIES TO BE INCULCATED	HABITS TO BE UPROOTED
Always speaking pleasantly, with respect, and with a smile	Speaking in rough language, using harsh or abusive words
Appreciating and encouraging others for their good deeds	Condemning and criticizing others
Speaking the right words at the right time	Arguing unnecessarily and giving advice without being asked
Expressing one's feeling or opinion to the concerned person in a nice manner	Back-biting
Always speaking the truth without fear	Lying and spreading rumors
Speaking after thinking, which involves self-examination and contemplation	Deceit and the habit of speaking without thinking
Seeing virtues in others	Finding faults in others
Making best use of time	Finding excuses to avoid work
Working hard and with devotion	Working carelessly
Always completing a job	Leaving things unfinished
Good hygiene, proper nutrition, and regular exercise for a healthy body	Bad hygiene, bad eating habits, and no exercise

15

DON'T SAY SOMETIMES 'YES' AND SOMETIMES 'NO'

Your child's health is in your hands

Parents are the first teachers of their children, while teachers are their second parents.

Your children's health is in your hands. They form their habits by watching you. How do our parents talk to each other at home, when do they get angry, what do they eat, how do they eat? Children notice all these things and then copy the same behavior.

If you want to see your children healthy, then you will have to break the habit of saying sometimes "yes" and sometimes "no." When an individual, after having said yes to something later says no, or says yes after having said no earlier, that individual loses people's trust.

When parents say "no" to their kids for something and later say "okay, fine, yes" when the kids stomp their feet and shriek, a bad habit begins to form in these kids. This is because the kids begin to realize that their parents' "no" can be changed to "yes" and vice versa. As a result, they start doing things as they please and thus lose their self-control. They also begin to learn manipulation, lying, and how not to fulfill their commitments.

That is why, before saying "no" to something, parents should think twice whether after saying "no" it will change to "yes" if the child starts acting out. If you are later going to change to "yes," then it is better to say yes right now. Similarly, if your "yes" is going to change to "no" later on, then it is always better to say no right now. In this way, the children will quickly learn that whenever you say "no," you do so after properly thinking over it and you mean it. This will teach the children to live in discipline. Once in a while, if you change your "yes" to "no" or vice versa, it is fine, but if every time your kids are successful in changing your decision, it spoils them.

Your young child is still raw and malleable. They don't know what they should eat and what they should not, and how much should they eat. When children eat too much ice cream or chocolate even when their parents tell them not to, they start losing their self-control and their health. It is difficult to learn self-control after growing up. That may be possible only if they meet a true spiritual master and follow the teachings. Otherwise, they will waste their lives in material pleasures and never attain the ultimate purpose of life. Today, the world needs kids who are disciplined, free from wrong beliefs, fearless, and brave, yet full of love and compassion. Those children, who will rise beyond their personal desires and become instrumental for raising the consciousness of the nation and the world, are the ones who will be called true and good human beings.

If parents tend to lie for every little thing, easily break their commitments, or end up eating more food when it's delicious, then their kids learn the same. Consequently, these kids are unable to imbibe honesty, reliability, self-restraint, and discipline in their lives. Therefore, parents need to create such an atmosphere at home that their image proves to be positive and inspiring for their kids.

No animal in their natural habitat needs discipline. It is only humans who need discipline because they destroy their health unconsciously. Diseases such as diabetes or hypertension do not affect any animal because they live a simple, natural life. When animals feel hungry, they eat, and only as much as needed. On the other hand, no matter how much you warn people having diabetes to avoid sugar, most of them secretly continue to eat sweets, which worsens their disease. This happens because man does not have control on his body. In spite of knowing that smoking and drinking are like poison to the body, people continue to consume these toxins. The only reason is that they have no discipline over their body. When children observe these behaviors from adults in the house, they also easily drift into these habits.

If you want to make your kids capable and healthy, you have to learn to control your mind. Because your child's health is in your hands, and your health is in the hands of your mind.

Train your children in such a way that when they grow up, they can proudly say, "My mother is like 'Mother Nature' and my father is my 'Father Friend.'

16

THE WORLD NEEDS WELL TRAINED CHILDREN

Recognize Your Child's Possibilities

What kind of children do you want?
Those that grow up fast, those that grow up slowly,
or those that grow up at their time?
Those children, who have been raised by the best parents in the right manner, grow up to perform great deeds for the world.

One may question, why is there a need for complete parenting? The answer is simple. Complete parenting leads to trained children. Trained children are the need of the world.

In India, November 14, the birthday of *Chacha Nehru* (Uncle Nehru) is celebrated as Children's Day. This day is an opportunity to recognize the potential of children and to enhance it. This is the day for every parent to contemplate how the right development and highest self-expression of their children can be brought about. If the person training the child does not have the right understanding, then the child will face difficulties and cannot progress ahead.

What kind of children do you want: the ones that grow fast, the ones that grow slow, or the ones that grow at their time?

If you are asked this question, what will be your answer? Once a child is born, they grow up in 15-20 years. If a drug is developed which makes a child grow up in 5 years, would you like that? Most people taking care of children want them to grow up fast.

The seed you sow today will grow into a tree. We usually do not plant trees that will yield fruit after 50 years, thinking, "This tree takes so much time to grow. Who knows whether we'll be here after so many years to enjoy its fruit." Likewise, some people think children take so much time to grow, and also it takes so much effort. Hence, most people would want children that grow up fast.

On the other hand, if you come to know that the tree which bears fruit after 50 years is going to benefit others for centuries to come, you may be ready to plant this tree. Children take time to grow, but we have to understand what they can do on growing up, what their possibilities are, and why it is essential to give time and care for them.

We should not think only about short-term benefits. We need to see long-term, what is going to happen down the years and down the ages. These very children will grow up and look after the nation and the world. Then how important it is to train them! If they grow up untrained, then what will be the state of the world?

If we want to take care of our kids in the right way, then we have to check what are the objects around them? What things will get in contact with them? For example, let us say you have a toy. That toy is such that it moves about everywhere and swallows everything it comes across, be it pebbles, metallic objects, or anything. On swallowing such things, its circuit and machinery gets damaged. If you aware of this fact, you check the entire area for any such objects lying around and remove them. A child is also like this toy.

Where does the child move around? What all are they seeing? What all are they hearing? Among those things, what are harmful for them? All of this needs to be taken into account because young children take in everything they come in contact with. Sometimes they imbibe such things that could be harmful for them. This applies to physical as well as intangible things.

Whatever the child would see, the parents have to see first. They need to know what the kids would think if they consumed so and so things, saw so and so things, or imbibed so and so beliefs. Parents have the responsibility of identifying what can be removed from the child's path and what cannot? And then, how to deal with what can be removed and that which cannot? If every parent feels the necessity of doing this, then raising children will be easier. We can create a new age.

If parents want their children to develop in the right way, then every parent will have to take up the role of a trainer. Every parent will have to train their children in a way that will enable them to easily learn and understand, and explore their highest potential.

If you want to clean the kitchen, you will first have to go to the kitchen. Only then can you clean it. In the same way, in order to train children correctly, you will have to first become a child and learn their language. Only then can you teach them effectively. Children learn in the language of stories and games, rather than directly being told what to do and what not to. Unfortunately, many parents do not teach and train their children in this way at all. It does not occur to them that these children can create a big revolution on growing up. If children are given proper training, taken care at the right time, given answers at the right time, encouraged to enhance their intrinsic qualities, given understanding to get rid of their shortcomings, they can achieve complete development. If they are given understanding before wrong tendencies develop in them, then after growing up they won't have to struggle with those tendencies. Every parent needs to help the children in this way, so that they in turn can help others.

Birth of tendencies or patterns in children

When something is said to young children, they give a certain response, and find some benefits of giving that response. They are not aware that if they continue to give that response every time, it will become their tendency or pattern. It is quite possible that this tendency will become a hindrance in their progress.

For example, a kid did some work for someone and got a chocolate in return or got to go to a movie. They feel nice about it. Henceforth, they expect the same kind of response for doing any work. This slowly becomes a tendency or pattern, which can prove to be very problematic.

That's why it is always essential to have communication with your children. Alert them at the right time and give the right answers to their questions. This will prevent the formation of these tendencies. When a tendency begins to develop in young children, they don't feel it would be harmful for them in the future. This is because they don't see any ill effects from it at present. In fact, they are not aware that a tendency or pattern is being formed. That is why, parents need to be alert about this.

What are our children seeing and hearing, and thereby what beliefs and assumptions are entering their minds? Consequently, which patterns and tendencies are forming in them? If these patterns are broken or stopped before they are fully formed, then every child will be free from wrong beliefs as well as from deceit. The purer the seed that the parents sow, the better will be the tree that grows. This tree will be of great service to the society, as it was raised in the right way. It has always been seen that the children, who are raised by right parents in the right manner, are the ones that go on to perform great deeds. They always contribute to the progress of the country and the world. But parents are the biggest contributors to the development of such children.

Children are very receptive and absorb everything. They don't know what is good and what is bad for them. Hence, it is essential to keep a watch on what is happening around them, as well as what and whom are they coming in contact with. If they are coming in contact with such things and such individuals who might cause harm to them or impede their progress, then keep your children away from them. At the same time, teach your kids about what is harmful for them and how to safeguard themselves against such negative elements, so that it doesn't hamper their progress.

The possibilities of today's children are very high. With time, children's understanding level is rising. They are learning everything very fast. Their capability is increasing. They lead their lives based on what they learn in their childhood, and their conviction grows on that teaching. Therefore, it is essential that only such elements be brought in contact with them that will make their life simple yet powerful and prevent them from forming wrong beliefs. This will be the right training for our children.

*As parents continue to converse with their children
and tell them stories,
children start opening up and feeling safe with them.*

17

CHILDREN SHOULD UNDERSTAND THE REAL MEANING OF FAILURE

Studies - an opportunity, not an adversity

A failure is not failure but a stepping stone.
To fail in something is not failure but to give up is.

Every success of the child becomes a cause of pride for the parents and raises their status. On the other hand, every failure of the child damages their status.

Grades or marks obtained by children should not become a status symbol for the parents. Once this happens, parents tend to put pressure on their kids. "You have to become an all-rounder… you should top in every subject… you should be a topper in every exam…" and so on. Due to this, the position of the parents wavers just like the throne of Lord Indra. If their child gets good grades, they feel their status is secure. If not, they feel their status is in danger. They feel this fear hovering over their heads all the time. Therefore, they need to decide whether they want to continue living with this fear all their lives or they should come out of it.

When parents say, "These are my kids," then just by saying "*my* kids" they get blindfolded. A parent thinks, "My kids should do this… they should not do that… they must get these particular grades…

they should not fail… they should do everything as I say…" This is where the trouble begins. If parents realize, "These kids have simply entered this world *through* us; they are on their own journey and we only have to help and support them," then their suffering will stop.

If parents let go of the sense of ownership toward their children and instead consider themselves as only their supporters, they will remain happy and so will the kids. In the future, when these kids achieve something worthwhile, they will be thanking their parents for allowing them to bloom fully and rise higher.

No little kid in this world feels bad on failing a class. In fact, they think, "Wow! I will be in the same class once again. I was studying right here last year, so I know everything. I'll be smarter than all the other kids in the class." They feel excited but parents shout and scold them, and they start feeling bad. They don't feel bad on failing. This is because the word 'failure' does not exist in the dictionary of children. Only when they grow up are they affected by the ailment of failure. However, failure is actually not failure. It is in fact a ladder that takes one toward higher growth.

It is observed in some kids that they are unable to accept even minor failures. In such cases, they need guidance. It is the parents who need to understand this and guide them at the right time. The first thing that should be clarified to children is that failure is not failure but a stepping stone toward progress. To fail in something is not failure but to give it up is failure. For instance, on getting less marks, if a kid says, "I will stop going to school from now on," then they move toward failure.

At such times, the child should be explained, "Getting less marks in one subject is not failure. Since you are growing older, now you have to work on more subjects. That's why there is a need to put in more efforts than before. Earlier, you had to manage only two subjects, but now it's four, and later it will be six. This is helping you to grow. Hence, it's essential to learn to convert failure into a ladder of growth."

You may have seen how a juggler smoothly juggles 3-4 balls at a time. He doesn't become an expert just like that. He carries out regular practice. Initially, he practices with only two balls and achieves success in it. Then he practices with three balls but one ball keeps falling repeatedly. He realizes his hands need more training. With some more practice, he is able to easily juggle three balls. Then he experiments with four balls at a time, in which he initially fails. In this way, he continues his practice and one day achieves mastery over it.

With this example, you may have understood that with every failure, you should learn your life lessons and move ahead. Every failure also implies that you need to train yourself some more. This is what you have to teach your children too.

Success lies hidden behind failure. Failing in one subject is no big deal, there is nothing bad about it. Such incidents become instrumental in boosting one's desire for achievement and ultimately one's self-confidence. Without being wavered by any failure in your life, you need to communicate to your kids a crucial lesson: "Failing in something is normal. Until and unless you pass through these incidents and become proficient in dealing with them, they will continue to reappear. Once you become proficient, all the best things in the world come to you because now you are working with the intention of becoming an expert. Therefore, just continue your practice and everything will solve in the process."

Create a platform for studies with your kids

When parents ask their kids to study, most kids say, "I know everything, I don't need to study." This makes the parents angry. The first thing you should understand is that if a certain situation is occurring repeatedly, then do not try to force the kid *during* that situation. When everything is cool and calm, that is the time when you should have a talk with your kids.

There is a need to create a communication platform with your kids. Otherwise, parents have a talk with their kids only when there is a problem. Before any such problem occurs, it is necessary to get together and create a platform. Make it a habit to talk to your kids daily. Ask them, how their studies are going on? What happened at school? Do they face any problems at school? If parents talk to their kids every day, then these problems won't even occur.

If parents create such a platform beforehand, it proves to be quite beneficial, because if the kid is not listening to you regarding a particular thing, you can talk it out and convince them. You can tell them how they can improve their studies and whatever else they are doing. You can also stress the importance of paying attention if the adults in the house are telling them something. It is crucial to teach your kids the importance of listening.

To make your children more amenable, you can teach them with examples from your own childhood. "When I was young, I too thought that I knew everything, but that wasn't the case. When questions were asked to me, then I realized that I don't know so many things. Let me also give you some questions, for which you can write down the answers. With this, you will come to know how much you know and how much you don't."

After discussing on this with the kids, decide on the times when you will give them such questions in order to test them. When you actually conduct such tests, their answers will either dissolve their misunderstanding or yours. Otherwise, for no reason, parents feel scared that their kids don't know anything.

Think about how you can create such a platform with your kids. When you share your own example with them, they understand that since you are speaking from your experience, they need to think about it. Kids want to learn too; they too want to understand; that is why they will take a step toward cooperating with you.

If you directly point out their flaws, without first creating a communication base with them, it's not going to work. "You don't do this task properly... you have done this wrong... you have done that wrong..." If this is what you throw at the kids, they wouldn't even want to talk to you. Because they know that as soon as you speak with them, you will indicate their shortcomings, so they run away from you. Hence, first create a platform with your kids, tell them some good things about them, and then they would be receptive for listening to you.

If the kids say they remember everything, then you can test them by asking some questions. Any misunderstanding, if present on either side, will give way to clarity. Otherwise, you will go on scolding them thinking that if they are not studying they are doing wrong. There is no need to live under a false impression.

The presence of the parents should help the kids to progress. You should praise them a lot and encourage them by saying, "You can do something different... you can do a lot of things... everything is possible for you because you have these qualities... work on enhancing these qualities... come, let us get together and discuss what all can be done to boost these qualities... we will help you in that..."

Children feel good on hearing that they have such qualities. Till a point of time, kids should definitely be showered with praises. After a certain point, they understand that, "Whether someone praises me or not, I am going to walk this path, and not waver from it." You only need to take care of them till that point.

*Your success is hidden
behind your failure.*

18

GOOD CHARACTER IN YOUTH IS THE NEED OF TODAY

Your goal, your efforts, your success

After the first mistake has occurred,
a second one occurs quite easily.
Hence, help the child learn
at the very first mistake.

To be a person of character means to understand that character is our greatest treasure and to lead our whole life based on this understanding. We need to develop our character and our children's character while carrying out our daily activities in such a way that no one would be able to shake it up.

In today's world, people's focus is mainly on material acquisitions such as expensive cars, beautiful houses, and other luxuries and comforts. The importance of building one's character is reducing day by day. If we can put in so much effort for building material things, then why not for building character? In fact, it is character that should be given the highest priority. It is the need of the hour. And, it's the need of today's youth.

Friends, as we know, play a big role in making or breaking one's character during one's youth. It is important to understand who one should befriend and who one should not. When an honest and intelligent boy becomes friends with another boy who habitually lies for every little thing, then in his company he too learns to lie. He says at home that he's going to college, but instead goes for parties, movies, and gets entangled in bad habits. This slowly corrupts his intelligence. He doesn't like to study anymore and begins to fail in his exams.

Going ahead, in order to maintain his bad habits and lifestyle, he needs money. So, whenever he needs some cash, he begins to lie and make some excuses before his parents and other family members, and takes money from them. Gradually, this goes to such an extent that he begins to steal. Slowly, it becomes a habit for him to lie about every little thing, due to which he eventually loses his credibility. Nobody trusts him anymore.

What this demonstrates is that after one mistake has occurred, the second one occurs quite easily. When one speaks a lie, they need lie a second time, and then a third time, and so on. In this way, young people get stuck in a negative cycle and their character is soiled by the lies and deceit.

Many times during youth, one fails to understand the fine line between the good and the bad. They rationalize and justify their wrong actions using logic. If they don't have something, they feel they are lacking it and feel embarrassed in front of others. "I don't have it. What would my friends think of me?" Such questions make their mind restless. Then, to achieve that object, they go to any extent, engage in deceit, and eventually ruin their lives.

In order to build their character, they need to stop relying on the crutches of greed and lies. Everything can come into their life without greed or lies; the only thing that is needed is honest thinking. Youth today need to self-examine honestly, and ask themselves, "What will I gain by speaking lies and what are the problems I could face due to this lies? What will happen due to my greed? If this behavior becomes my habit, then what complications is it going to create for me and my family?"

Lying for every little thing is a wrong tendency, and kids carelessly go on deepening this pattern in their everyday interactions. Unfortunately, they have to face the consequences in the future.

There is no shortcut to success

Young people with weak character dream about completing their work without putting in any effort. Not only are they afraid of hard work, but they also want quick success using shortcuts. Very often, they don't even hesitate to take the support of corruption, hatred, and wrong people.

> A college professor entered the class to conduct the last year biology exam. He addressed his students. "It was a pleasure teaching you this semester. If you pass this exam, you can go to medical college. Seeing your hard work throughout this term, I am offering you a proposal. Those who don't want to give this exam, they will receive a 'B' grade without appearing for the exam."
>
> Most of the students were ecstatic on hearing this. They gladly accepted the professor's proposal and left the class. The professor asked the remaining few students in the class, "Does anyone else want to go? This is the last chance." One more student left the class.
>
> Then the professor closed the door and noted down the names of the remaining students. He said, "I am happy to see that you guys believe in your capability. Hence, I am giving you an 'A' without even appearing for the exam."

The students who had left the class earlier were pleased to take the shortcut because they could avoid giving the exam and still get a 'B' for free. The students who stayed back, took the long cut (which is actually the normal cut), and chose the path of hard work. As a result, they got an 'A'.

Young people whose character is not strong enough consider money to be the only ladder of growth and the final goal. They also tell others that using their skills and talent they should collect as much money as possible. They start accumulating comforts and luxuries using money acquired by wrong means. Their life is lost in the pursuit of sensory pleasures.

Every young adult should know that to achieve true success, what is needed is not a shortcut but persistent effort in the right direction. Hence, to strengthen their character, the youth have to reduce their desire for convenience and give priority to their capability and hard work.

In order to invest their capability and hard work at the right place, they first need to decide the goal of their life. By deciding their goal, every problem of the youth can be solved—be it laziness, boredom, money management, team work issues, or time management. Once they decide their priorities, everything will start falling in place.

John Wooden has said, "Ability may get you to the top, but it takes character to keep you there." There are many people who want to reach the peak of success using their physical beauty. Some of them are successful in doing so, but they lose their purity of mind in the process. Due to power but no wisdom, they are unable to maintain their purity of mind. Such youth are able to gain success but end up losing their wealth of character.

The one whose mind is not pure, their character also cannot stay pure. On the other hand, there are some people who are unable to climb the peak of success but they have purity of mind and wealth of character, hence they achieve success in the true sense.

The time has come to start teaching the importance of character to today's generation right from school and college, so that they are able to set the right goal for themselves and earn the wealth of character and values.

We can achieve eveything even without greed and lies.
The only thing required is honest thinking.

*Two trains can run together on parallel tracks
but their journeys are different.
Much in the same way,
your child is on its journey alongside yours.
Allow them to be on their journey.
Support them to learn their lessons.*

Eradicate These Four Negatives

1. Problems related to children
2. Anger related to children
3. Parenting myths
4. Doubts and queries regarding children

19

PROBLEMS RELATED TO CHILDREN

10 Steps to Awaken Self-Esteem in Children

*Don't feel bad if you cannot give
expensive toys to your kids.
But do give them love and self-confidence.
This will build up their self-esteem.*

Many parents think that if they give the child lots of love and affection, the child will get spoilt. But the fact is that the child does not get spoilt by love but by force and pressure. This, however, does not mean that you should always let the children do whatever they like or always give them expensive toys and clothes.

The meaning of love here is that your behavior with your children is such that it builds a healthy self-esteem in them. And they are able to give you what they have received from you—true love, unconditional love. Give such love to your kids. Let it become clear to them right in their childhood that, come what may, your love for them will never diminish. Only then will they fully open up and blossom. They will attain their highest goal of life; attaining which is their nature.

Self-esteem means the self-image of the child—what the child thinks of himself or herself. In order to build a healthy self-esteem, they need the following ten qualities:

1) **Self-confidence:** The confidence to accomplish a given project, however difficult it may be.

2) **Respect:** Respect for oneself and others with the understanding that every being in this universe has been created by one supreme power.

3) **Fearlessness:** The courage to do what one is scared of.

4) **Excellence:** Becoming an expert in at least one field.

5) **Leadership:** Trying for the development of all the surrounding children.

6) **Decision-making:** Taking decisions at the right time and completing the tasks.

7) **Willpower:** Resolving and finishing work within the decided time, whatever be the obstacles.

8) **Information:** Always collecting all the information related to the work at hand.

9) **Aim:** Always working with an aim in mind.

10) **Hard Work:** Never shirking from hard work.

How will these ten qualities develop in children? It is again the parents who will have to take the initiative. In fact, they will need to first cultivate these qualities in themselves and become a role model for their children. Only then can they give the highest training to their children, which will help them develop self-confidence.

Only from self-esteem is self-confidence created. If the self-esteem of the child is to be improved, then parents will have to improve their own self-esteem first. The following points will help parents to develop self-esteem:

1) First accept yourself as you are.

2) Identify your weaknesses.

3) Don't be scared of your weaknesses and don't hide them.

4) Consider your weaknesses as a challenge and work on them.

5) Imbibe patience and dedication in your life.

Children of those parents who imbibe these qualities progress better and faster because these parents establish a good relationship with their children. Such parents are fully aware that when children progress, their parents progress too. Training of children becomes the training of the parents. They know that being blessed with a child in itself means that they too have to become a child. Complete parents know that when children are learning, they are bound to make mistakes, but they ensure that the same mistake does not occur repeatedly.

Complete parents prepare today for whatever is to be done tomorrow. They do it well and with awareness. They figure that only then will tomorrow's work be completed in the best manner. Therefore, if our children's tomorrow, their future, their life is to be filled with happiness, then it is important to prepare for it today itself.

Relationship changes with time

Remember that the child's relationship with the parents changes with time. Shower love and affection on your children until they are 5 years old. Give them lots of praise until they are 10 years old. Praise them at the right time and also punish them at the right time. But after the age of 16, develop a relation of friendship with them.

If your children have problems such as the ones listed below, their solutions too lie with you. If with time you feel a change in the behavior of your kids, you too will have to change your behavior accordingly. You will have to give them what they need at a given time. Let's take a look at some of the problems you could be facing with your kids and what could be the probable causes.

A) If your child does not listen to you (disobedience):

1. Are you expecting too much from them?
2. Are you stopping them from doing something they want to?
3. They want to feel their individuality, they want to feel free, due to which they want to do some things in their own way and see how it turns out.

B) If your child is using bad language:

1. Are people around them (siblings, neighbors, friends, teachers, etc.) using bad language?
2. Are they learning this from people with whom they like to hang out and are they doing this in order to please them? Examine this possibility and pull out this bad habit from the root.

C) If your child is moody:

1. Are they under some stress or suffering from depression?
2. Are they suffering from lack of sleep?
3. Is it anxiety due to exams?
4. Did they have a fight with someone?
5. Is it that they don't have a goal to aspire and work toward?

D) If your child throws things around (untidiness):

1. Keep in mind that once a kid has learned to keep things properly, you need to let them do it themselves. Never try to do it for them. Do not rearrange what they have done.

2. Is it that their school, house, friends, or teachers have changed?

E) If your child is found stealing something:

1. Is the atmosphere at home very strict?
2. Are they feeling jealous of children who possess certain objects and they don't?
3. Are they hanging out with the wrong crowd?
4. Are they feeling lack of love from their parents?

F) If your child is not eating properly or has some eating problem:

1. Is it that they don't like themselves? Are they harboring some kind of guilt?
2. Is it that they don't like the food served to them?
3. Are they feeling lack of love?

G) If your child is lazy:

1. Do they lack motivation and inspiration?
2. They may not be interested in the work they are doing.
3. They may be having some health problems.
4. Their school, house, friends, or teachers may have changed.

H) If your child is lying:

1. Are they scared of being punished?
2. Are their needs not being fulfilled?
3. Are they in bad company?

4. Is lying a habit that they have developed?

5. Are parents making their kids speak lies (on phone or to guests at the door)?

All the above points need to be reflected upon. You can then safeguard your kids from them.

Accept your child as is

Many parents burden their children with their own expectations and ambitions. They tell their kids, "I wanted to become an engineer but couldn't. So, now you should become one." Or, "There has not been a single doctor in our family, so now you have to become a doctor." In this way, parents impose their desires on their children. Giving a goal to your child is good. But it is also necessary to see whether your child's body-mind is suited for it. Does the child have the capacity for it? Does the child want to become that? Does the child have the primary qualities to become a doctor or an engineer? Because, it has often been seen that the child has the qualities and creativity of an artist, but the parents want to make them a doctor. Now the child that has become a doctor to fulfill the parent's wishes, how will he or she be able to make their inner talent shine? If they have been forced to become a doctor, to what extent can they do justice to this profession? This is because an artist is lying dormant within them. They cannot become a good artist, but neither can they become a good doctor.

When children grow up and achieve their goals after studying in their field of interest, they also become good human beings. Therefore, we should keep in mind what do we want our child to become—just a doctor or engineer, or a good human being. If your children have the qualities of a doctor or an engineer, and study in that field, then they will certainly become one. But for them to become good human beings, it is necessary to develop certain qualities in them.

How is our interaction and behavior with our children? *We should behave with children in the way we want them to behave with us.* This applies not only to our children but also to our behavior with our family, our relatives, our society, and everyone else. Our children learn from how we handle our relationships. Let's take a look at an example that illustrates this point.

> There was a family in which the grandparents, mom, dad, and a child all lived under one roof in a nice house. One day, the child came running excitedly to his parents and said, "Mom, Dad, look, I have drawn a picture. This is a bungalow, which I am going to build when I grow up." Mom and Dad loved the drawing and asked further about the picture, "What is this and what is that?" The child explained, "This is the living room, this is the kitchen, this is the bathroom, and this is my bedroom." Dad asked him, "And where is our bedroom?" The child said, "A bedroom for you?! You haven't made a bedroom for grandma and grandpa. Then why should I make one for you two?"

Children speak what they see. Thus, it is very important to pay attention to our behavior in front of our children and with our children. They learn and grow up observing our behavior.

Children don't learn from what we say.
They learn from what we do.

20

ANGER RELATED TO CHILDREN

Don't get angry unconsciously

Anger causes unconsciousness.
Unconsciousness gives rise to wrong beliefs.
Due to wrong beliefs, we forget our true nature.
On forgetting our true nature, anger becomes destructive.

When children are very young, they need attention and security. They get it from their parents. In fact, everyone takes care of them during their childhood. They get whatever they want and whenever they want it. That is why, unknowingly, they begin to feel that they are the most important people in the world. Actually they are not aware that they are the weakest and hence are being given the maximum care and attention.

In this way, children begin to mistake their weakness to be their superiority. With this misunderstanding, they begin to get things done from others, which eventually makes them adamant in nature. Then, if some of their demands are not met, they begin to get angry thinking, "All my demands get fulfilled, then why not this one?" They need to understand that it is not necessary to be stubborn and furious. They need to realize that they are delicate and hence are being given full attention, so that they can grow up well. The moment they understand this, they will be grateful.

Only the human baby needs more attention. Otherwise, they may not survive. The young ones of animals do not need much attention and can grow up by themselves. Due to this, anger, hatred, and malice do not develop in them. But such feelings do develop in the human offspring. In this way, the feeling of anger begins in childhood itself.

Children gradually learn that they just have to get angry in order to get what they want. But before that, they learn to cry, and then they learn language. Thereafter, they observe how others use anger to get their demands fulfilled. They watch the language and expressions being used by their siblings and neighbors and think that's the only way to get things done.

Solution for Parents: Right conversation with children

Unfortunately, parents are equally responsible for the child getting angry as the child itself. When children get livid, most parents tell them, "You are such an angry kid. What you are doing is totally wrong." This makes the kids feel guilty and they start developing an inferiority complex. The parents don't try to understand why the child is behaving angrily. They are not able to talk to the child about this. It is often seen there is very little conversation between the child and the parents. Sometimes, there is no conversation at all. In such cases, where the kids are unable to speak what is inside them, their feelings burst out in the form of rage.

Some parents are not aware that their behavior with the children needs to change according to age. When the children are young, they should be treated in a certain way. When they grow up, interaction and communication with them has to be in a different manner.

As children grow, their requirements will increase and so will their learning. Many questions will arise in their minds. Some of their questions will be answered and some will not. Some of their desires will get fulfilled and some will not. Anger arises in them when their desires are not fulfilled. Such a state appears in children when there is something missing in their upbringing. In fact, anger is a manifestation of lack of communication. Hence, it is critical for parents to learn the art of communicating properly with children. This solution is absolutely essential for proper upbringing of children.

Alertness of Parents

When the child gets angry, parents can teach them, "You don't need to get angry. You can get what you want even without anger." Create such an environment in your home where your children get the full opportunity to say what they want to. They should be able to easily communicate their needs. This will enable you to develop a relationship of friendship with them.

In every home, conversation should take place between parents and children every day. Consider this as an essential part of your daily activities. It will prove to be very beneficial for your family. Misunderstandings will reduce, relations will grow stronger, and friendship will develop between family members.

Every parent needs to be aware of how to handle children when they get angry. In fact, anger is also a method of communication. It is used as a method of expressing displeasure when one doesn't know other ways of doing so. If children learn the art of expressing themselves by some other way, they will realize there's no need of anger. They can easily get what they want by using other methods. If we all learn the knack of presenting our views, anger can be eliminated. Anger is just a feeling or a method of expressing a suppressed desire.

After a certain age and even after attaining maturity, if someone keeps getting angry, then they themselves are responsible for it. When they know that they get angry due to some weaknesses, and yet they don't try to overcome those weaknesses or learn from them, then they are only encouraging their anger. In this case, they will never get rid of anger.

Getting Angry Consciously

Suppose a child has done something wrong. The parents get angry but don't lose control. They consciously decide that they should use their anger for improving the child, so that he or she doesn't repeat that mistake. So, they take action with full awareness that, "Now I am going to punish the child." This is getting angry consciously. On the other hand, if a parent first lashes out at the child and later on gives a reason that it was for their own good, then this is getting angry unconsciously and unawarely. They try to justify their anger by giving a reason.

Anger can be used consciously, but only when necessary. In this case, anger is not a disease, but a necessity, a need of the hour. For example, if a little kid puts her hand in fire, it is necessary to show anger. But it should be used with full awareness and carefulness so as not to harm the child in any way. Thus, being aware during anger is the greatest remedy for anger.

There is a huge possibility for development in a child.
To become a child again after growing up
is the last stage of development.

21

PARENTING MYTHS

Don't Raise Kids with Wrong Beliefs but with Understanding

With one matchstick of supreme wisdom,
all wrong beliefs can be annihilated
and total freedom can be achieved.

A belief is something we assume to be true. Some beliefs could actually be true, while some may not, which are then referred to as wrong beliefs, false notions, or myths. Wrong beliefs are wrong impressions and assumptions. They are something that the mind believes but which are not the truth. They appear to be true because everyone around us believes in them. That's why we too begin to believe in them. For example, somebody tells us that if a cat crosses our path, it is a bad omen. Or the number 13 is unlucky. We believe them and live with that thought in our mind. But there are no proper reasons for these beliefs.

There was a writer who gathered all the negative incidents that happened in the world on the 13th day of the month and published them. Due to this, millions of people started considering the 13th as an unlucky date. But the same can be done with any other date because negative events are occurring in the world on every date—be it murder, theft, violence, or any other crime. In the same way, on every date many good events also take place, such as inventions, donations, opening of orphanages and other institutions, death of criminals, birth of a saint, and so forth. Dates are neither good nor bad. They are made good or bad by our thoughts and false beliefs.

There are some beliefs that were consciously created by our ancestors who were intelligent people. They created these beliefs considering the time, weather, situation, and the need of that time. Some of those beliefs have become outdated as time has changed, while there still could be some beliefs that are worth following. But if you follow them, do it with awareness and understanding and not out of blind belief or fear.

Five such beliefs related to children (mostly followed in India) are presented below. Understand them and follow them with awareness. For some reason, if you are unable to follow any of these on some day, there is no need to feel scared or get carried into any kind of doubts or blind beliefs.

1. **One should not cross over a baby**

    This belief came into being because:

a. Babies are very delicate. They cannot express their pain, nor can they show where it hurts. If someone accidentally steps on the hand or leg of a baby wrapped in a blanket, it could be dangerous. Besides, dust from the person's feet crossing the baby can be harmful for it.

b. While walking across the infant, there is a possibility that one may drop some object that they are holding on the infant.

2. **One should not rock an empty cradle**

    This belief was created because if we rock an empty cradle, there is a tendency to give it a brisk and rapid swing. Other children could use it as a toy. Thereby, the cradle could become weak at its hinges, which could be risky for the baby. In order to avoid this situation, the belief was introduced that one should rock the cradle only when there is a child in it.

3. A baby's hair should not be combed for a year

A baby's scalp is delicate and a comb has pointed teeth, which can harm the scalp. Hence, this belief was introduced.

4. It is essential to shave a child's head

This belief was introduced for two reasons:

a. After the first growth of hair is removed, the new hair that grows is thicker and denser. In this way, the hair on the child's head develops properly.

b. After shaving, the circulation of blood in the entire head increases. Due to this, the brain of the child becomes sharper.

Keeping in mind these two reasons, a custom was introduced to offer the child's hair to a deity in a temple, which is called *Mundan* ceremony.

5. A black spot should be marked on the child's face for protection from envious eyes

The thinking behind this belief was that sometimes when people see a lovely object or a beautiful child, jealousy arises in their mind (especially in those who don't have a child or that object). This jealousy could turn to malice. To protect something from malice, an ugly thing is often attached to it. In India, a black doll is often hung in front of a beautiful house. It is man's nature to first find faults or to see any shortcomings. The black doll or the black spot or a black string tied around the child's neck distracts people's attention. This belief was introduced for the safety of children and in order to guard them from others' jealousy.

Let us next consider some global beliefs. There are some gender based myths that influence parents such as "Boy's should be dressed in blue and girls in pink" or "Ballet and gymnastics are not for boys!" It is easy to understand that these are mere generalizations and therefore may not be true. But there may be many deep rooted myths. Listed below are some deep-rooted myths that you may be carrying in your mind as a parent. Ask yourself, do you consider these statements to be true? These wrong beliefs may actually be limiting your ability to be a great parent. How many of these do you subscribe to?

Myth #1: The child is too young to understand anything. You don't have to take the child seriously. Children don't get hurt emotionally.

Reality: *Children are very sensitive and understand things we say. Be mindful of what you say to them.*

Let us understand this with an example. A boy hears his mother say, "Today some relatives are going to visit us. Be at your best behavior." Later on, the boy sees those relatives arriving. He is impressed. After a few days, his mother says, "It's going to rain tonight." It rains that night and the child is impressed once again. He concludes that whatever his mom says is true. He believes her words and actions to be always true. One day, the child does something wrong (according to his mother). Mom scolds him and says, "You are hopeless and good for nothing." The child believes her. He always remembers these words. He grows up with lack of confidence and is always subdued. He never makes his own decisions and lives a depressed life.

While it is true that one should not physically harm a child, many parents end up causing far more dangerous emotional harm. As parents, we must safeguard our children from both physical and emotional hurt.

Myth #2: I will love my child the way I never received love / I will love my child exactly how my parents loved me.

Reality: *The needs of every child are different.*

Every child has their own 'love bank' and needs it to be full every moment. Some children like to be cuddled by their parents. Their parents' touch makes them feel comfortable and secure. Some children want parents to play with them. They feel loved when their parents are present around them. Others need gifts. They love to be with their toys and gadgets. Some kids like to gain and share knowledge with parents. They keep on asking questions. We should know what type of kid we have. If we try to shape them in our own limited ways of thinking, they might resist or get subdued. Their possibilities may never be explored. Your perception of what your child needs might be different from what the child truly needs. Understand your child's need and accordingly give them what they need.

Myth #3: A father must not be very strict with his children. A mother should not give too much love to her children.

Reality: *Both tough love and soft love are required.*

If one were to look at the roles that nature intends us to play, a father is supposed to give the child the hardware (hard training) and a mother is supposed to give the software (soft love). Both tough love and soft love are required to make them complete individuals.

Myth #4: Parenting is tough and the hardest job in the world. It is better to not be a parent or commit to parenting. What is the point of parenting when your children don't care for you when they grow up?

Reality: *Parenting is a divine task of shaping the character of a child.*

Parenting is a selfless and enjoyable task of giving to the world someone who will make the world an even better place. Parenting is a way to uncover and manifest the qualities of compassion, care, patience, and so many other virtues in you. The very purpose of parenting is to awaken and release the unconditional love lying dormant within you.

Myth #5: The primary responsibility of a parent is academic growth of the child.

Reality: *The primary responsibility of a parent is to cultivate or pass on good values to their children.*

Put character building over everything else. A child is like a white board. Parents are like markers that write on the board. The child will act and live life according to what is written on the board. While academic excellence should be one of the key aspects of your child's growth, the most important responsibility of a parent is to show them the path to holistic growth based on good values so that they become a complete person.

Myth #6: Teach your children spiritual values and morality from a young age by telling them and explaining to them about the scriptures.

Reality: *Don't teach spirituality to your children, demonstrate it.*

The best thing you can give your children is the gift of happiness and peace. Let your children see how you take decisions with inner peace and how you act with inner poise. This will be transferred to them. Giving children spiritual instructions at a very young age may confuse them.

If you want to instruct them, then instruct them on self-development. Teach them concentration, willpower, focus, communication, etc. Talk to them about strength, stamina, and taking initiative.

Verbalize skills for your children, but let them internalize spiritual wisdom by observing you.

Parents leave a lasting impression of their actions on the child. The child is a photocopy of the parents in many ways. Children replicate what they observe. Every moment, children absorb some part of the actions, words, behavioral patterns, and habits of their parents, relatives, and teachers. Little children are not capable of analyzing and contemplating, and therefore, in ignorance they accept these observations as facts. Imagine what image the children will try to create when they become parents. They will fill their children with the same beliefs and myths they lived with all their lives. They will transfer all their patterns and tendencies to their children. The child does not know right from wrong in their actions. A child thinks whatever parents do is the right thing and the right way to live.

Myth #7: I am responsible for bringing my children into this world, and therefore, I have to worry about them.

Reality: *A parent's concern for a child is natural, but it should not turn into worry.*

Let your concern be a positive concern, not worry. When you tackle life's challenges with happiness, knowing that it is God's will, and these challenges have appeared in your life to make you stronger and wiser, you become a magnet and attract the best things in your life. When you worry unnecessarily, you invite the worst in yours as well as your children's life. Always remember: "Your children come *through* you, not *from* you." They are God's children and so are you. Take care of them with joy and faith.

Myth #8: Being a parent, it is more important to spend time with our children rather than spending time in spiritual activities.

Reality: *The best gift a parent can give to the child is to be free of* *wrong beliefs, myths, tendencies, and patterns.*

Spirituality will help you get rid of all your negative traits. Spending time on spiritual growth is part of effective parenting.

Myth #9: I must ensure my children have access to the best education and become intelligent and smart.

Reality: *While it is right to want the best education for your children, still better is to teach them the art of learning.*

When children learn the art of learning, they will explore greater heights in life. The art of learning can then be applied to not only academics but other aspects of life, such as social, physical, emotional, financial, and spiritual, all of which together leads to a complete life. Teach your children how to learn and show them how to lead a spiritual and moral life through your actions. There cannot be a better gift than teaching your children to achieve liberation from sorrow and to attain their ultimate purpose on Earth.

Myth #10: To fulfill our duty as parents, all we need to do is send our children to a good school; provide for their food, clothing and shelter, take them to their sports practice or dance class, and take them on one or two vacations a year.

Reality: *These are things every parent should strive to provide. However, beyond all this, every parent should teach children the values to be a good person and a responsible citizen.*

Children are most influenced by the emotional attachment they feel with their parents and other family members. A good education, sports, safe environment in a good neighborhood, and vacations are something that every child will appreciate and enjoy. However, the most important thing a child yearns for is the love, affection, trust, and confidence of their family members, especially their parents.

22
DOUBTS AND QUERIES RELATED TO CHILDREN

Frequently Asked Questions by Parents

Problems that don't kill us, make us stronger.
Doubts that make us think, make us wiser.

In this chapter, we will take a look at some of the questions frequently asked by parents who attend sessions in Tej Gyan Foundation, and the answers given by spiritual master Sirshree.

Q.1. Why do good parents get bad children and bad parents get good children?

What is your definition of 'good parents'? If good parents have got bad children, the question is how do the kids become bad? What good did you see in the parents? Did you find it good that the parents gave everything that their children asked for? Children said, "I want this" and immediately they were given those things. The child said, "I will not eat this and I won't eat that" and parents said, "Ok. Fine." By seeing this behavior of the parents, do you feel, "How good these parents are! They fulfill all the wishes of the child." This is not the definition of good parents. This is what has spoilt the child. On the other hand, it also doesn't mean that parents who fulfill all the wishes of their kids are not good.

The true definition of 'good parents' is those parents that are wise and possess the knowledge of right parenting. If parents are wise, their children cannot be bad.

How do children become good? This depends on their upbringing, whether it includes the right amount of everything—love, appreciation, right guidance, discipline, etc.

It is important to give children at the right time the right appreciation or the right punishment if they do something wrong. This means that love, praise, and punishment should not be more than necessary and should be given at the right time. It should not happen that the child did something wrong today and you punished the child after some days. That will be of no use. What's the benefit if you try to discipline the kids after they have got spoilt? Also, the right amount is important. When we add salt to food, it has to be in the right quantity, it has to be only how much is required. Only then the food tastes good. Hence the significance of right quantity.

Also, never give such punishment that will prove to be detrimental for the child. For example, "Today you will only study mathematics the whole day." You may feel you have given the right punishment. But it's not right because if math is boring for the child, how will they do it the whole day? They will only begin to hate studies. When studies begin to feel like punishment, how will they do it throughout their education? Hence, it is essential to give the right punishment in the right amount at the right time. In the same way, it is also essential to give them the right appreciation and encouragement at the right time. It is then that kids become good, otherwise they get spoilt. With such upbringing, the child will become a leader with effective leadership qualities.

Often, outsiders may feel, "These parents are so good! They give whatever the child asks for." But did the child really want what was given? The child actually wanted to spend time with mom and dad but instead was given some more toys. Then are these 'good parents' in the true sense? The children want their parents to chat with them, help them in their studies, do drawing and craft with them, and take part in their discussions. Only through such upbringing will children become good.

Every child is different and so is their definition of love. Parents come to know what type their children are and what fills their love bank through proper communication. Parents may feel that if they give expensive toys and gifts to their child, they have done their job. But what does the child want? The child may be yearning for a few loving words and a pat on the back.

The father says, "I have done everything for these kids. I bought them this, I bought them that, I got them into a good school." But the children say they did not get what they wanted. If the father had spoken to the kids and understood their actual needs, then the kids would have definitely turned out to be good children. Whenever you feel why good parents get bad children, think about all these factors. Don't blame it as the fruit of bad karma of your past lives. Pay attention to your present patterns. Dig deep and discover what your tendencies are. Ask yourself, "How was I brought up by my parents? What tendencies came to me from their genes? If the same have appeared in my children too, then how should I raise them so that they become free from those tendencies?"

Those children will be called lucky whose parents behave with them like 'Bright' or 'Complete' parents. Bright parents know they should not make their kids study out of fear. Studies should not feel like a punishment. They understand how to train a child and what the child wants from them. If the child wants loving words, then give them loving words and not gifts. If they want gifts, then your words will have no effect. If the child wants your loving touch, then it is necessary to touch your child, hug them and pat them lovingly. When children are given what they need at a given time, then they progress easily. Some children want time, so it should be given to them. They want their parents to be with them, play with them, and have fun with them. If this does not happen, they think, "We too will do the same with our parents." We will need to understand the mentality of our child. If this understanding is present, then good parents will certainly get good children. Hence, the definition of good parents has been stated here.

Then, what is the definition of 'bad' parents? How do bad parents get good children? Let's understand this. Those children who have got bad parents reflect deeply on how parents should **not** be. They contemplate, "We should not become like this." They are able to see how unhappy they are because of their parent's conduct. Therefore, they become good. Thus, when you see bad parents, never assume that their children will also turn out to be bad. Some children have the habit of contemplation right from the beginning and they do things differently from others.

It is important to understand both the definitions properly. It is not that if parents do "this," that's why they are good, or parents do "that," that's why they are bad. The reality is that those parents are good who act according to the need of their child, which helps the child to progress.

Q.2. Does the subconscious mind function in a child of 2–2½ years?

Yes, the subconscious mind as well as the unconscious mind of a child is always functioning. The child starts learning right from the time it's in the womb, but this learning is not in words. As soon as the child is born, how is the surrounding environment? Is it comfortable or not? Does the child get its mother's lap? At this age, they need their mother more than anything else. This is because they feel more secure with her, as they had been safe in her womb for a long time. As soon as they are away from her for a little while, they want to be near her again. If they cannot, they get frightened internally, which means the fear begins in their subconscious mind. Hence, the mother should always be close to the child. Some people leave their children in orphanages. In such children, many confusions arise and their subconscious mind catches some fears in childhood itself. Hence the need for a mother. A mother is always there. Whenever the child cries, she is there. At this time, it is crucial to pay attention to what the child needs. The child's mind records everything. The impact of every record is seen on their life when they grow up.

Q.3. How do average people raise a child and how do 'Bright' parents?

Children have come through you. Give them the opportunity to become what they can. Give them the opportunity to make mistakes. Always be present to help them. They are becoming instrumental for you to express your love. If you have love within you, then you need a chance to express it. If there is love, then there needs to be a receiver too. Even the receiver is important. If the clouds are filled with water, they *will* rain. Children are giving you the opportunity to shower the love filled in your heart.

'Bright' parents will take it as an opportunity. Such service will begin to take place through them where there is no ulterior motive. Like, some people think, "I could not become a doctor, so my child should become one… There is no doctor in our family, so our child should become one." These are some of their *reasons*. Bright parents possess the understanding that they will not make the child into something due to such *reasons*. They will let the child become what it wants to.

Bright parents fully understand what is the divine play going on in this world, then if the child gets worried or troubled due to any reason, they can guide the child in the right way. They know they should always be present when children require them and give them what they need, because children will give to others only what they get. Children who grow up with abuse may become successful. But what will they give others? Most probably the same abuse. They become insensitive to others' pain. Don't kill their sensitivity. They should be able to feel everything and not become rigid. Let them always be open to new things and not lead constricted lives. Let them look at things from a new angle. All parents should create such opportunities for children.

Q.4. Can parents make their children positive and equanimous (*satvaguni*) in childhood itself?

Yes, children can be and should be made positive and equanimous in childhood itself. Parents have to see what habits should be developed in their kids in their early years, which will increase their self-confidence and willpower. In other words, whatever your children decide, they should be able to do it. If they decide to wake up early in the morning, and they are able to do it, this enhances their self-confidence. This discipline over their body that they learn benefits them a lot in their life. If you have to instill such habits in your child, you will have to set an example for them. You too will have to wake up early. Thus, you will have to walk every step with your child.

'Deciding something and then carrying it out without fail' – this discipline is going to be highly useful in their future. Such children when they decide to achieve something (because they want it and not because somebody is forcing them to), they definitely achieve it. This strengthens their willpower. This means they are able to do whatever they decide. This very habit also helps them to get rid of ignorance and wrong beliefs, which in turn makes them positive and equanimous.

Q.5. When children don't listen to me, I get very angry and lose control over my mind. I am always in control at other times, but only in this case, I lose it. What should I do?

Till date, whenever you have expressed anger, what have the results been? Did the children improve? Understand from this that the children are giving you an opportunity to observe your anger. When you get this opportunity, then watch the anger that has arisen and check, "What is exactly happening with me?"

Do express your anger where necessary. It's not being said that you should not get angry. Showing anger may sometimes yield good results, but it should not get out of control. Do not go into extremes. When angry, some parents just don't let it go, while some others don't talk to their kids at all. This should be avoided. Remain balanced.

Some parents keep getting angry on their children throughout the day. The children begin to get immune to their anger thinking this is how their parents always behave. If you *have to* show anger, do it just once or twice and in a proper way, so that it has the right effect on children. You can decide in your mind and express anger once in a day. But before that ask yourself, "Have I exhausted all other means? Have I tried to make them understand in loving words?" Because to do so, you have to think. In order to avoid thinking, we immediately get angry in unconsciousness.

Thinking increases awareness. With increasing awareness, even before rebuking your child, you will ask yourself, "Am I aware that I am rebuking him? Is it necessary to do this?" If there is no other remedy, then do it. If you reprimand them with understanding, it is fine. If it is in the interest of the child, and if the child gets disciplined, then it is necessary. On growing up, they will thank you for it.

A scolding at the right time prevents you from screaming at the child often and is also very effective. If the child is commended at the right time, then they progress rapidly. When we don't do the right things at the right time, we end up screaming at the child. Every parent should note this and increase their level of consciousness. The most important point to remember is that right decisions begin to take place only when your level of consciousness rises. Then you will begin to get answers from within you as to what is right and what is wrong.

Q.6. Will thinking about children, worrying about them, getting angry, and then trying to explain them, take us away from the supreme truth?

Think about children and become a child yourself. Whenever you scold your child, you usually think in your mind that it was essential to do so. But certainly ask yourself, "Did I think this before scolding or after?" If you thought before, then it is right. If you thought after, it is wrong. If after scolding or hitting the child in anger, you feel, "This was necessary and that's why I did it," then this will only serve to increase your ego. If you know beforehand that the child will not understand without getting angry on him, then get angry, and do it so vigorously that you won't have to do it again. Of course, this has to be at the right time and in the right measure. If your intention is pure, then you can do it.

But is it the case that you are not doing your homework? By 'homework' it means are you giving enough time to your children? Do you talk with them about things that are essential? Do you ever ask your child, "How do you feel when I get angry with you for some reason? Do you feel it is right or not?" If you ask this to your child, they may surprise you with their answers. You may have never imagined that a child could think so much. You will also discover what they think about you, which you were completely unaware of.

Most often, parents are not aware of the child's feelings. They do something only when the child does something wrong. Even when the child isn't doing anything wrong on being left alone, they can be taught so many things with stories and examples. You can portray how a kid in the story suffers because of doing something wrong. Parents should do their homework on what shortcomings the child has and tell him stories accordingly. On making him understand in this manner and asking him what he thinks, he will himself come out saying that it was necessary to scold the kid in the story. First understand the child and accordingly make them understand. Then they too will believe that you are their well-wishers. In this way, when a common platform is created, then nothing can go wrong. Also keep in mind that the child should not develop fear or an inferiority complex due to your reprimands and punishments.

Thus, a child helps you break many of your wrong patterns and develop good qualities. They become instrumental in awakening the divine attributes lying dormant inside you. They can help you to become a child again. Thus, they don't take you away from the truth but toward it.

Q.7. Whenever my children don't listen to me or neglect their studies, I get stressed and start shouting at them. What is the best method to control my shouting?

First ask yourself that till date what have been the benefits of your shouting on them? If your kids are improving because of it and they have benefitted in any way, then go ahead and shout at them. In fact, you will *have to* do this for your children. On the other hand, if you notice that the kids are getting desensitized to your voice, then they will not pay much attention to it. They will think you always keep shouting and it's your habit. The impact of your shouting will go on reducing.

This way you are harming yourself and also the kids. First understand why we shout. We shout because we want a result. If we want a good response from the child, then will we get it? Ponder on this question. Will we get it by shouting at them or proving them wrong? Or are there other methods? Can we try some other experiment? Many new experiments are possible. You have to work toward improving your understanding. Some contemplation is needed in this regard.

Regarding what should you do to control yourself while shouting, there is no question of doing anything when you are shouting. People always ask, "What should I do when I get angry?" They are told not to do anything at that time. Whatever needs to be done, has to be done much earlier. You need to prepare for it beforehand. When thirsty, a person should not ask questions like "Should I dig a well?" You need to dig a well much before you feel thirsty. If you feel that you are prone to get angry often, then prepare for it well in advance. When angry, your brain doesn't work. You cannot think of anything. Only words or actions burst out. You are just not aware at that time.

Therefore, you should start working on yourself when you are in a normal mood. Try small experiments. When you succeed in those, you'll be able to succeed in bigger experiments. Ask yourself much earlier, "When anger arises in me, what is the desire behind it? Which desire is being hampered due to which I feel angry?" This is one of the causes of anger; we get angry when our desire is not fulfilled. All parents want that their child to study and top the class. But is this possible? How can every child top the class? What do parents want? Why do all parents want to take their child in just one direction? Reflect on these questions. You need to gain some understanding as to what you are going to do when you get angry? Which means you have to practice self-enquiry, contemplation, and meditation well in advance.

If you have been meditating upon this in a calm environment and when you are not angry, then it can be expected that you will remember this mediation when you feel angry. If you are unable to do it in a good atmosphere, then how will you do it during anger? Start practicing when all is well. When you feel all is going well, then understand that it's time for meditation. People feel that meditation should be done when things go wrong. It's just the opposite. You should work upon it when everything is going on smoothly.

When you are calm and you have the opportunity, carry out self-enquiry with honesty. "Who am I in reality? Whatever thoughts are appearing at this time, to whom are they appearing? From where are they emerging? What are these thoughts informing me about?" Contemplate this. If this contemplation continues, then there is a possibility that when you are angry, you will remember who you actually are. Then anger will become instrumental in reminding you of your true divine nature. Later you will thank anger saying, "It's good that anger arises because it enabled me to know about my true self. I worked on anger so much." Anger is energy. Learn to use it.

Q.8. How should we teach a 3–4 year old child?

There are two methods of teaching a child.

First method: Teach them using right brain techniques

Little children don't understand directly many things that we want to explain to them. That's why the way you teach them should be very simple. Children learn faster through their right brain. Hence, teach them using right brain techniques, which include stories, colors, pictures, charts, graphs, maps, sounds, games, plays, spelling words using hands, going from whole to a part, and so forth. When they are telling you or showing you something new or are doing things correctly, pay attention to them, praise them generously, and encourage them. This straightaway teaches them that they need to do things like they are doing now. This is good for his progress.

Second method: Teaching through demonstration

Demonstrate to children whatever you want to teach them. Behave with children in the same manner that you want to see them behave. Speak to the children in the same way that you expect them to speak. Children are constantly in contact with you and keep watching you carefully: How emotional you get when you are saying something? In which situation you get angry? When do you feel happy? The child is learning all this from you. The child observes how emotional you get even on a small matter and how you speak in that state. They even observe when you say something without emotion. For example, when someone does something and you shout, "Why did you do this?!" The emotion of anger gets across. But if you say the same thing calmly, "Hey kiddo, why did you do this?" The calmness and ease with which it is said gets across. If you explain to your child normally and without getting emotional, the child is able to understand more clearly.

Since children learn by observing you, so you have to be alert and aware of what you are doing and what are your kids learning from your behavior? Let's consider a few examples.

1. A father after returning from the office starts playing drums but asks his kids to do their homework. What would they learn from this behavior? If you want your kids to study, then you will have to pick up something to study or read too and sit along with your kids. When they see their parents sitting nearby and reading or doing some work, they begin to study

too. Unfortunately, you cannot think that you have returned from the office, your job is done, and you can just sit and relax. If you think like that, then your kids can say, "I too went to school. Why am I not allowed to chill? Why are you forcing me to finish my homework right now?" That's why, whatever parents want their child to do, they have to do it first and lead by example.

2. If parents talk to their children discourteously but demand their children to speak to them with respect, then the kids find themselves in a dilemma between the two types of behaviors. It takes a long time for children to understand such things. When a father catches his son smoking a cigarette, he starts shouting and may even hit the boy. Due to this stress, the father pulls out a cigarette from his pocket and starts smoking. On seeing this contrary behavior, the boy is astonished. "He got mad at me for smoking, and now he's doing the same!"

3. Many times, when an older brother hits his younger brother, the father in turn hits him saying, "You should never hit anyone younger to you. Your brother is smaller than you, don't take advantage of him." The older brother wonders, "But dad just did the same thing! He hit me even though I am smaller than him." The older boy does not understand the difference between the two beatings. In the same way, a father shouts at his daughter and says, "Don't shout." The girl is baffled seeing her father shout at her while asking her not to shout.

4. If you thank you kids for even little things that they do, they too will learn to give you thanks and respect. For instance, your kid brings you a glass of water and you thank them. They feel very happy to be acknowledged for such a small thing. Soon, they too begin to thank when someone does something for them. For example, when their mom prepares their lunch box

and readies their school bag, they begin to thank their mother. They realize that their mother does so much for them and they learn to appreciate it. When you do certain things in front of your kids, the same habits seep into them.

On the other hand, if you tell your kid, "It's your duty to give me water... you should do it," the child is unable to understand something like duty. But if you thank them, they surely feel good. The next time, when you ask your kid to bring you a glass of water, they will happily run and bring it for you.

In this way, parents should be able to thank their kids for everything they do. Recognize and feel all the blessings you have been bestowed with. If someone is doing something for you, you should be able to appreciate it and express your thanks. If you want to inculcate this habit in your kids right from childhood, then you need to thank them every time. Even if the children do nothing big, just something small, and yet receive thanks, they feel so good. "I did something, for which I was thanked." A feeling of joy arises in them.

5. When talking to your kids, always use words that make them feel good. When children are blamed for everything and reproached every time, "*You* did this... *you* did that...," a feeling of guilt develops in them. They start making the same mistakes in fear repeatedly. That is why parents should always use respectful words while speaking to their kids. It should not be assumed that it is only kids who should respect the parents, while parents should only pass orders. You need to talk to children respectfully, so that they can learn to do the same with you and others. If words such as 'sorry' or 'thanks' never come out of your mouth, then the children too will not learn these words. Even after growing up, they are never able to utter such essential words.

6. If children don't learn to give respect to their elders, then on become adults, they find it really difficult to bow down in front of someone even to receive blessings. It feels like punishment to them because the habit of giving respect is not inculcated in them since their childhood. When children see their parents taking blessings from their parents, soon they too learn this habit. If parents don't respect their elders, then kids mimic their behavior. Then parents wonder why their kid does not respect them. Although these may appear minor, but parents should demonstrate all these things in order to train their children.

7. If parents rise early in the morning, then children become early risers too.

8. If parents have self-control and switch off the television once the show they were watching is over, then the kid too learns to do the same. If you demonstrate self-control, only then your children will imbibe this quality. If you are unable to exercise self-control while watching television, you may even consider getting the cable connection removed altogether.

You may say, "Why aren't we allowed to do a little of this and a little of that?" That's because then your kids will emulate the same behavior. All the good habits that you want your kids to learn, you will have to cultivate them in yourself first. This may be difficult for you, but you need to do it in order to give a good upbringing and complete training to your children.

You might say, "Why do *we* need to learn these things now? We have done all this when we were students." But your kids don't understand what all you have done during your student life. They want to see you doing it in front of them. They feel, "If this thing is difficult for my parents, then it's difficult for me too." That's why, you will have to demonstrate these qualities in you for the growth of your child. If you give time to your hobbies and interests, your kids will also want to spend time on their hobbies. If you want your kids to exercise, you will have to exercise with them. When children see their parents doing certain things, they imitate them. It then becomes easy for them to learn and carry out those actions.

Do not consider your children as objects.
Consider them as the living consciousness,
which is inside every living being;
that we also call as God.

*If parents cannot forgive their children's mistakes,
the kids grow up with a feeling of guilt.
If children are given unconditional love and time,
they too will be able to give
unconditional love to others.
In this way, they learn
a very important lesson from you.*

Three Final Important Suggestions

1. Importance of teachers in a child's life
2. Importance of meditation and prayer
3. Importance of 'Bright Parents'

23
IMPORTANCE OF TEACHERS IN A CHILD'S LIFE
A Noble Profession

Children progress by using their imagination.
We don't have to hinder their imagination
but we have to safeguard them
from harming themselves in the process.

Parents are the first teachers of children, and the teachers are their second parents. Thus, the role of teachers cannot be overemphasized. They have a deep and lasting impression on a child's life.

The first duty of a teacher is to get children interested in those subjects in which they are weak. They can combine the subject with a game and teach it in a creative way. If every teacher learns this art or they first study and practice how they are going to teach the children, then every subject can become interesting for kids.

So far, the biggest mistake that has been seen in schools is that the teachers study their subject repeatedly and reach a high level. Then it becomes difficult for them to come down to the level of children. They talk to students from their high level. Hence, children are not able to understand, which math formula is the teacher talking about? Which principle of science are they teaching? At that time, teachers forget that children can understand better if the teacher comes down to their level and explains. For example, a teacher reads the dictionary, picks up some difficult words, and uses those in his speech, thinking that everyone will feel he is intelligent and more educated than others. The fact is that students cannot understand him easily. Thus, it is essential for teachers to get down to the level of children while teaching them. The purpose should be that children should learn what is being taught. In this way, the teacher too learns the art of teaching.

Children use their right brain

Children learn with their right brain, while adults (parents, teachers, etc.) use the left brain. Adults use logic. Although parents and teachers too used their right brain during their childhood, but with time they forget about it.

It is vital for teachers to also use the right brain once again for the children. They need to relearn all those things that they had once learnt in their younger years. They will have to remember how to learn in a new way through the right brain. Thereby, they will be able to teach children in a way through which they will get the expected results from the kids.

It is crucial to first develop an interest for studies in children. Until this happens, children will always find it troublesome to listen to difficult subjects. Teachers also need to understand that they should not just teach the syllabus but also add other important topics. For example, how to progress internally and externally, the art of observation, meditation, concentration, experimentation, creativity, communication skills, social skills, kindness, helping others, etc.

Why is Teachers Day celebrated?

Teachers Day is celebrated to remind and remember the role and responsibility of teachers in the growth of students. In many schools, students play the role of teachers on this day. When playing this role, they realize how troublesome it is for teachers when students play mischief or make noise in the class.

For example, a little girl used to trouble her mother to no end when her mother would try to feed her. In order to teach her the right lesson, the mother one day suggested that they swap their roles. She told the girl, "You play the role of mommy, while I will be your daughter." When parents play such games with their children, not only the kids feel good but they also learn some things. When the girl acted like her mother and began to feed the daughter (actually her mother), she said, "I am not going to eat." She then ran around the house in order to avoid food. The girl too had to run behind her to feed her. During this game, the girl soon realized the trouble that her mother went through every single day. This brought a change in her behavior from the very next day. This is a good way to teach your kids.

Seeing their parents, an awakening should take place in children. It is the duty of all parents to make their children aware of the ultimate purpose of life. Until and unless children understand why they should study and what is the actual purpose of studies, they wouldn't want to study. Why are examinations conducted? Unless the purpose behind the exams is made clear to the kids, they will continue to fear exams. Hence, parents should make their children aware of the true purpose of life. This understanding should be imparted to kids that all the qualities they develop during their student life are going to be useful for them in the future for the expression of their highest self.

The tradition of *gurukul*

In the olden times, children used to stay in a *gurukul* under the guidance of a guru right from childhood till the age of 25. They learned everything in the gurukul. How to work for a living? What exactly is wealth? How are children born? What is a householder's life like? What kind of self-expression is the purpose behind everything that we learn and do? Why has the world been created, why have we been created, and what's the ultimate purpose behind everything in our life? And so on.

In this way, these students spent 25 years in the ashram to become 'Bright householders.' A special environment was available in the gurukul to inculcate these essential teachings of life. This environment also protected the students from the lures of the material world. People in those times knew the importance of shielding the children up to a certain age, till they were ready to step into the world and begin their lives as 'Bright householders.'

Consider a little sapling that has just emerged from the ground. It is vulnerable. An animal could eat it, a strong wind could uproot it, or a human could stamp on it. Almost anything could destroy it. The sapling needs safety and security for some period of time, in the form of a fence around it.

Likewise, when small children go to school, what kind of protection do they need? In the olden times, people knew the importance of keeping children safe. They understood the true purpose behind everything they did. They were aware of the ultimate purpose of life. They knew how someone can become a Buddha or a Meera. What is the purpose of this education? Why have we come to Earth? What is the secret of living a truly happy and successful life? Students gained all this knowledge in the gurukul so that they could live like a lotus in this world. A lotus flower lives in water, thrives in water, but doesn't allow even a single drop to stick to it. In the same way, how can we live in this world and carry out our duties, while still being detached? How can we express our true, highest self? What kind of inspiration can we become for people around us? All this training was given to students during their time in the gurukul.

Unfortunately, today such systems are not available. If they are, they are not fully effective due to heavy population and many other problems of the present world. But whatever we can do for our kids today, it is important that we do it. We need to contemplate how alongside regular studies, children can be imparted the wisdom of life. Children should be trained keeping the end goal in mind. They should be taught to not consider exams as something to be feared but as the means to develop the qualities that will help them to achieve the ultimate purpose of life.

If children are made to understand that we all are essentially the students of life and the students of God, it could completely change the way they learn and study! They will start learning from nature, from life, and from everything.

In ignorance, people think the profession of a teacher is merely a job, a small job, and there is nothing special about it. In reality, it's a noble profession, it's pure and sacred work. Teachers can bring about the highest growth of a person, a society, a country, and the world at large.

Parents and teachers team

There is a need to create a common platform between parents, teachers, and children. To achieve this, teachers and parents should regularly exchange information about the kids. This communication is crucial for the safety and progress of children. Parents should observe how the things that the children learn from school are influencing them. And the teacher should openly and honestly inform parents if their children are behaving according to what they have learnt or seen at home. Such communication will help in the child's growth.

In the olden days, everyone possessed this knowledge. The gurukul system was created by self-realized souls. Today, if that facility is not available, we all need to think what is the least that can be done in the present circumstances. To create a highly evolved world, along with parents, the role of teachers is also critical.

Teacher vs 'Bright teacher'

A teacher teaches the students to observe, while a Bright teacher teaches how to observe without attachment or identification. A teacher teaches how to study, while a Bright teacher teaches how to study without becoming arrogant. Otherwise, as children learn and accumulate more and more knowledge, their ego gets bigger, and they start thinking, "I know this… I know that… People don't know this…" They consider knowledge as wisdom and boast about it. Hence, a Bright teacher teaches how to gain knowledge and wisdom without becoming egoistic.

A teacher gives information to the students. What all is going on at various places in the world? How many countries are there? How many oceans are there? What is produced where? Thus, a teacher informs the students all about the world. Whereas, a Bright teacher teaches the students what's going on in the world as well as what should be going on in the world but isn't. A Bright teacher raises the awareness of the students and makes them understand how so many things are still waiting to manifest in this world due to unconsciousness and lack of knowledge of supreme truth. Therefore, Bright teachers emphasize to their students the importance of this knowledge and how it should reach everyone as soon as possible, so that those higher things can manifest on Earth.

When someone hears such knowledge, they would like to apply it in their lives and raise their level of consciousness. If you don't know what all things are waiting to manifest and haven't yet appeared, how can you have thoughts in that direction? No one really ponders on this topic, hence the need of Bright teachers who can contemplate it and can tell students what all can happen in this world but is not happening. This will cause a surge of inspiration in people to take on this goal and work on it.

If every school has such Bright teachers, they will talk about this with the students. A desire to fulfill that goal may arise in someone, which will cause a major change in the world. Otherwise, how big is the desire of an average person? On the other hand, the love of supreme truth and wisdom can make one perform miracles, which can result in transformation of our planet.

It is very important for children today to receive this knowledge. A teacher's profession is indeed a noble one. Individuals in this profession should be aware that they are not in it only to make a living. When a highly evolved world gets created on Earth, those who assume the role of teachers at that time will be raising the consciousness of people and hence will be the ones who would be paid the highest salaries. Those teachers would fully understand the importance of the role they have chosen. They would know that they are going to carry out the most important work in the world. While those who will be paying them would know that this money would only be utilized for the highest development of their children.

All those who are teachers today can at least ensure that they are not connected to this profession just to earn a living. They should consider it as sacred work just as that of a doctor. If someone is about to become a doctor, they should ask themselves, "Am I joining this profession simply because it will fetch more income? Or am I really going to give to the society and the world what this profession can give?" These kind of reminders and resolutions can work wonders.

If teachers understand the nobility of their role, then how should they work in this profession? That training should be given to teachers. For example, if a teacher does not love mathematics, his students too will not love it. Math will always be a difficult subject for them. Often, students share that they had a good math teacher and hence they always had interest in that subject. Those who did not get a good teacher always complain that they simply cannot grasp this subject and it's the reason for their failure.

This means that when teachers love the subject they teach, they will arouse the interest of their students in that subject. They will also ensure that weak students don't fall behind. They will take extra classes for them to first arouse their interest. Bright teachers make even difficult subjects interesting. For example, instead of explaining several formulae in an hour, they teach just two formulae and let the students play around with those, by asking, "Let's see how this formula is created in the first place? What the inventor of this formula must have thought? What are the tricks one can use to make it easy?" In this way, when children begin to play with those formulae, they start developing interest in that subject. And when this is practiced repeatedly, then they too begin to love the subject.

In this way, when parents and teachers work together, children can progress with great speed. When these children grow up to realize how many troubles they have been saved from due to the training they received, they will thank their parents and teachers.

If anything negative happens with children who don't get proper training during their childhood, they get very upset. Children who receive proper training and right guidance at the right time develop self-confidence within them. When these confident children face an adverse situation in their lives, not only are they calm but they also comfort and support others by saying, "We will find a solution. There is definitely a way out of this problem. The only thing is that we should think calmly and positively." They are able to do this only due to their right training. Today, you will find only a few kids in society who have a positive outlook. It is an extremely important attribute and all children should have it. For that, parents will need to give them the best training.

Chances are you did not receive such training either before you became parents. But now you are fully aware, mature, and receiving this training, so you should take its full benefit. If we are getting rid of all our wrong tendencies and habits, and continuously improving ourselves, then there is a chance that the mistakes that we have committed won't creep into our next generation.

Writing a diary is a beautiful habit for self-development. Write down all the tasks and challenges that you plan to undertake for your own and your children's progress in your diary.

24
IMPORTANCE OF PRAYER AND MEDITATION IN CHILDREN'S LIFE
Learn and teach

There is great power in prayer.
Prayer can cool the fire of worry and even soften a stone.
It can stop a storm and bring a drowning ship to shore.

There was a school where children were also taught prayers, and as part of their homework, they were instructed to pray every night before going to bed. One day, they were taught a prayer which included the line, "Dear God, I will never lie or deceive." The next day, the teacher asked the students, "Did you say the prayer I taught you yesterday?" One child said that he did not. He was reprimanded for this answer. If that child had lied and said he had prayed, then he would not have been admonished.

Is it not worth pondering here that the child was speaking the truth? The prayer is already seeping into his life and he *is* praying in the true sense. Is prayer called a prayer only when uttered by the mouth? When the teacher did not understand this, she scolded the child. The child starts thinking that he got reprimanded on telling the truth, so it's better to lie. That way he will escape the punishment as well as he need not pray. In this manner, the beginning of prayer itself takes place on the wrong note. The purpose should be that prayer should permeate their lives and not become just homework.

How can our prayers be fulfilled? When does prayer not yield results? How does prayer work? Reflect on these and other questions on prayer, and see for yourself the miracle of the power of prayer in your life.

In fact, it has so much power that even one prayer can set you on the path of supreme truth. Everything in the world can be changed through prayer. Even doctors advice prayer as the only resort in the final stages. Many times, we hear doctors say, "This patient was not going to survive, but we don't know how he made it." The point is that even today such incidents are happening that were not supposed to happen. The reason behind this is that somebody's prayer is constantly working for that incident to take place.

Whenever adversity and worry torments you, remember this law of nature: *"Before giving a problem, its solution has been given to you."* In other words, you are given a solution first and then the problem. Just as nature has already arranged for milk before a child is born. You only need to *find* the solution, which is already within you. Prayer helps in bringing out that solution, that answer. If we don't use such a great power as prayer and choose to remain stuck in our ego, it would indeed be foolish.

Teach your children to meditate and pray right from childhood. This habit will become a *Brahmastra* (infallible and greatest tool) in their future. If parents themselves do not have this habit, then they need to cultivate it for the sake of their children. Six examples of prayer and one meditation technique have been presented below. You can use these or any other prayer that you may have been practicing.

1. **The following prayer can be offered on waking up in the morning:**

    Dear God, thank you for showing me a new day once again.
      You have given me another chance to praise you.

Dear God! Today this temple opened at 6 o'clock
(say the time you woke up).
Let this temple (your body) be clean and pure throughout the day.
Let the bells ringing in this temple
help in raising the feeling of devotion in the people around me.
Thank you for fulfilling my prayer.

2. **This prayer can be said before commencing your daily routine:**

Dear God! Please give me the power to understand
what I can change and what I cannot.
Give me the strength to change what I can
and the strength and patience to withstand what I cannot.

OR

Oh my God! Give me nothing but your love and blessings.
Your love and blessings will automatically beget
everything that I need.
Thank you… thank you… thank you.

3. **This prayer can be said before meals:**

When you sit to have a meal, close your eyes for two minutes and bring before your eyes and give thanks to all those who were responsible for bringing this food to you.

Thank you to the farmer who grew this crop.
Thank you to nature that provided sunlight and rain.
Thank you to the people who sold this food.
Thank you to the person or myself who brought this food to this place.

Thank you to the person who prepared this food.
And thank you God for giving me hunger
so that I can satiate it and enjoy the feeling of gratification.

4. **Say this prayer before going to sleep:**

    Dear God! Thank you for making my day so good,
    I was able to remain happy throughout the day.
    Kindly bless my night too.
    A thousand thanks for all your blessings.

5. **Say this prayer when you are about to begin a new job:**

    I am God's child. My success is ASSURED.

6. **Say this if fear troubles you:**

    I am God's property. No evil can TOUCH me.

Breathing Meditation:

This meditation technique is easy to practice for children and beneficial for adults too.

1. Sit straight on a chair or on the floor in *sukhasana* or *padmasana*.

2. Take one or two deep breaths, breathe out slowly and let go of all your tension.

3. Thereafter, continue breathing naturally. Whether it is short breaths or deep breaths, let them continue naturally and easily. Do not try to control your breathing.

4. Feel your breath go in and go out. Let your mind be aware of the breath going in and out.

5. The breath passed through the right nostril… or through the left nostril… or it passed through both nostrils… keep noticing

it. Be aware of every direction and every state (warm or cold) of your breath.

6. Focus your mind on the incoming and outgoing breath. (This enables the fidgety and restless mind of kids to calm down and settle, which improves their concentration in studies.)

7. Sometimes your breath may be short and sometimes long. Keeping the body still, notice every inhalation and exhalation.

8. If your mind strays, then as soon as you realize it, bring it back on your breathing. In this way, by consistently practicing this meditation every day, you will succeed in mastering it.

9. Gradually increase the duration of this meditation. Meditate for 10-45 minutes at your convenience. You can practice it and then teach your kids to practice it with you.

25
IMPORTANCE OF BECOMING BRIGHT PARENTS
Householders – Monks – Bright Householders

Small children are always in the experience of Self, where they do not consider themselves as the body.

Householder

The aim of a householder is to enjoy the pleasures of this world. A householder earns money to enjoy the luxuries of life as much as possible. While going through the hardships of earning, if sometimes they fail to make money, they feel angry, miserable, and suffer a lot. They feel happy only on acquiring money. They don't hesitate to fight with relatives or friends for the sake of wealth.

They become attached to those who help them. They get married. They worry about their name and fame all the time. They are happy when respected and furious if insulted. Then they have kids. Later on, there are conflicts with kids. Overall, after going through the pains and pleasures of life, a householder bids farewell to this world. They never get the thought: Is this all life is about? Being born, growing up, getting married, raising kids, getting old, and dying? The same mundane things repeating daily—the same old quarrels, the same anger, the same thoughts of jealousy and envy, the same greed, and so on? They never feel real happiness in their life. They never come to know the real purpose of life.

Monk

Exactly opposite to a householder is a monk who has turned his back to the world. They believe there is no point of living in this kind of world. They have hatred toward the society. They believe that since they lived as monks, they would get a direct pass to heaven after their death. But they live with hate in their heart for all householders. They have the same anger; they haven't got rid of it. They don't run toward but run away from wealth. They choose this kind of life because they fear hell and desire heaven.

A householder is greedy for worldly possessions, while a monk is greedy for heaven. Actually, there is no difference between the two. The lives of both are based on greed.

Bright Householder

A Bright Householder does not live in greed. They live with the understanding of why they have come to this world and what is the purpose of their life. They are aware of their ultimate goal. They know they have to play whatever role has been given to them in this world. And while fulfilling their duties that the role entails, they also have to work toward their ultimate purpose, which is to realize their real, formless, limitless self and express their divine qualities.

Hence, they are not affected by anger, fear, or worry. They don't feel envy, jealousy, greed, hatred, or guilt. They live a simple life. They don't have to deliberately practice 'acceptance,' since acceptance is a natural flowering of the understanding of truth they have attained. Due to the feeling of acceptance, they never feel sad or miserable. If they ever get angry, their anger is merely an act. It does not touch them inside. Such anger is in fact beautiful, creative, and constructive. It does not destroy anything but creates. Their anger is for the good of the society, the country, and the world, because it contains no ill-will, malice, hatred, or jealousy. Their actions arise from their intuitive mind and higher self, none of their actions are reactions to people or situations.

They do not harbor worldly desires but only the auspicious desire to realize and express their true divine self for the good of all. This desire is beyond all the other desires, hence a Bright householder is never affected by sorrow. Sorrow lives in that mind which sustains and thrives on desires. It's ironic that a monk renounces the world but is unable to renounce his desires. The monk turns his back to the world and to his duties, in order to achieve heaven and liberation. Whereas Bright householders live in the world and fulfill all their duties, yet do not get attached to anything. They remain detached and unbound. They don't renounce their desires for the sake of another desire; they completely give up the attachment with all desires. That's why, they don't have to work on getting rid of anger. It automatically fades from their life.

A Bright householder progressively becomes free from reacting. That does not mean that they never get angry. They do but only where it's necessary. They turn everything in their life into a stepping-stone toward their ultimate goal. They use anger in the same way. If anger has arisen, they know how to utilize it for their own good as well as the good of others.

A Bright householder is one who has surrendered to God. They say to God, "If you have given me strength, it's you who will make me carry out actions. And whatever you make me do, I will do. I have no desire of my own, no will of my own. Your desire is my desire. Thy will be done."

Qualities of a Bright householder:

1. Unshakable faith:

The first and foremost quality of a Bright householder is unshakable faith, which does not waiver in any situation. This faith is not some blind faith arising from ignorance, but from the understanding of supreme truth. Bright householders look at every event with the torch of understanding and use it for the higher purpose of life. They have experienced the all-pervading God or Consciousness. They know that the God or nature that has given them birth will also take care of them till the end. They have this conviction and hence their prayers have power. Every moment, this faith provides them the right guidance and the right information. That is why, their faith does not waiver even if negative-appearing events occur. They not only learn from such situations but also know the actual purpose behind them. They know the secret of the whole universe.

2. Flexible intellect:

Flexible intellect is that which can mold itself to every place and every situation. A Bright householder behaves as a child with a child, as an old man with an old man, as a youth with a youth, as a man with a man, and as a woman with a woman. There is such flexibility in their life. They first become a role model and then teach their children.

The plants that stand upright during storms are uprooted and destroyed, whereas the ones that are flexible and easily bend (like grass) survive easily. Similarly, people often lose love and respect in relationships due to their ego and haughtiness. Bright householders know how to bend and adjust when required. This is not related to ego but stems from their understanding.

They know that anger and fear are harmful for them in the first place.

3. **Fearless eyes:**

Bright householders have fearless eyes and courage, and hence they do not fear problems. On the contrary, problems fear them and offer them a gift before leaving.

Each one of us can have such fearless eyes and limitless courage. The only thing needed is the understanding that will dawn through systematic listening of the supreme truth. If some fear lurks inside us, then how can courage enter our lives? Fear of death is a fairly common example.

The purpose behind the fear of death ingrained in each individual is so that we don't try to escape life by committing suicide as soon as we face some hardships. The concept of death is explained to kids early in their childhood. We can get rid of this fear too when we truly understand what is death and what is life. Life is perpetual and goes on even after death. Thus, death is not actually death (the end). With full knowledge of death, Bright householders lose the fear of death and enjoy a 'Bright' life, which is beyond life and death.

* * *

You can send your opinion or feedback on this book to:

Tej Gyan Foundation, Pimpri Colony, P. O. Box 25,
Pimpri, Pune – 411017 (Maharashtra), INDIA.
email: mail@tejgyan.com

THANKS

All the contents of this book have been compiled from the discourses delivered by Sirshree. It contains the answers given by Sirshree to the questions asked by seekers related to children and parenting. We would like to extend our heartfelt thanks to Sirshree and the seekers.

The goal of Tej Gyan Foundation is that all the families of the world should become 'Bright householders.' 'Bright parents' will raise their children in such a way that these children will become instrumental in the progress of the world to a higher level.

In this book, some points are mentioned in brief. Tej Gyan Foundation conducts training programs on this subject. These training programs are conducted in the form of: *Abhay Vardaan Shivir (Gift of Courage for Kids), Mini Maha-Aasmani Retreat for Teens, Inner 90 for Youth (Value Education), Family Shivir,* and *Parenting Seminar.* Till date, many families have benefited from them. You can too, as they will help you to understand this subject in depth. Higher knowledge and highly effective techniques are taught in these seminars and retreats for children and parents. Everyone wants to become an ideal parent. Training is given in depth about how to develop the qualities that you need to become ideal parents. Besides this, there are books available on other topics too for yours and your children's complete growth. For further details, please contact Tejgyan Global Foundation.

About Sirshree

(Symbol of Acceptance)

Sirshree's spiritual quest which began during his childhood, led him on a journey through various schools of thought and meditation practices. His overpowering desire to attain the truth made him relinquish his teaching job. After a long period of contemplation, his spiritual quest culminated in the attainment of the ultimate truth. Sirshree says, **"All paths that lead to the truth begin differently, but end in the same way—with understanding. Understanding is the whole thing. Listening to this understanding is enough to attain the truth."**

Sirshree is the author of several spiritual books. His books have been translated in more than 10 languages and published by leading publishers such as Penguin and Hay House. He is the founder of Tej Gyan Foundation, a not-for-profit organization committed to raising mass consciousness by spreading "Happy Thoughts" with branches in the United States, India, Europe and Asia-Pacific. Sirshree's retreats have transformed the lives of thousands and his teachings have inspired various social initiatives for raising global consciousness.

His works include more than 100 books and 3000 discourses. Various luminaries and celebrities such as His Holiness the Dalai Lama, publishers Mr. Reid Tracy and Ms. Tami Simon and yoga master Dr. B. K. S Iyengar have released Sirshree's books and lauded his work. 'The Source' book series, authored by Sirshree, has sold more than 10 million copies in 5 years. His book *The Warrior's Mirror*, published by Penguin, was featured in the Limca Book of Records for being released on the same day in 11 languages.

Tejgyan... The Road Ahead
What is Tejgyan?

Tejgyan is the existential wisdom of the ultimate truth, which is beyond duality. In today's world, there are people who feel disharmony and are desperately trying to achieve balance in an unpredictable life. Tejgyan helps them in harmonizing with their true nature, the Self, thereby restoring balance in all aspects of their life.

And then there are those who are successful but feel a sense of emptiness or void within. Tejgyan provides them fulfillment and helps them to embark on a journey toward self-realization. There are others who feel lost and are seeking the meaning of life. Tejgyan helps them to realize the true purpose of human life.

All this is possible with Tejgyan due to a very simple reason. The experience of the ultimate truth is always available. The direct experience of this truth is possible provided the right method is known. Tejgyan is that method, that understanding. At Tej Gyan Foundation, Sirshree imparts this understanding through a System for Wisdom – a series of retreats that guides participants step by step

Magic of Ultimate Awakening Retreat

Magic of Ultimate Awakening is the flagship self-realization retreat offered by Tej Gyan Foundation The retreat is conducted in two languages – Hindi and English. The teachings of the retreat are non-denominational (secular).

This residential retreat is held for 3-5 days at the foundation's MaNaN Ashram amidst the glory of mountains and the pristine beauty of nature. This ashram is located at the outskirts of the city of Pune in India, and is well connected by air, road and rail. The retreat is also held at other centres of Tej Gyan Foundation across the world.

Participate in the *Magic of Ultimate Awakening* retreat to attain ageless wisdom through a unique simple 'System for Wisdom' so that you can:

1. Live from pure and still presence allowing the natural qualities of consciousness, viz. peace, love, joy, compassion, abundance and creativity to manifest.
2. Acquire simple tools to use in everyday life which help quieten the chattering mind, revealing your true nature.
3. Get practical techniques to access pure presence at will and connect to the source of all answers (the inner guru).
4. Discover missing links in practices of meditation *(dhyana)*, action *(karma)*, wisdom *(gyana)* and devotion *(bhakti)*.
5. Understand the nature of your body-mind mechanism to attain freedom from tendencies and patterns.
6. Learn practical methods to shift from mind-centred living to consciousness-centred living.

For retreats, contact +919921008060 or email: mail@tejgyan.com

A Mini retreat is also conducted, especially for teens (14-17 years) during summer and winter vacations

Write for Us

We welcome writers, translators and editors to join our team. If you would like to volunteer, please email us at: englishbooks@tejgyan.org or call : +91 90110 10963 or +91 90110 13207

MaNaN Ashram

Survey No. 43, Sanas Nagar, Nandoshi gaon, Kirkatwadi Phata, Sinhagad Road, Dist. Pune 411024, Maharashtra, India.

About Tej Gyan Foundation

Tej Gyan Foundation (TGF) was established with the mission of creating a highly evolved society through all-round self development of every individual that transforms all the facets of his/her life. It is a non-profit organization founded on the teachings of Sirshree. The foundation has received the ISO certification (ISO 9001:2015) for its system of imparting wisdom. It has centres all across India as well as in other countries. The motto of Tej Gyan Foundation is 'Happy Thoughts'.

TGF is creating a highly evolved society through:

1. Tejgyan Programs (Retreats, Courses, Television and Radio Programs, Podcasts)
2. Tejgyan Products (Books, Tapes, Audio/Video CDs)
3. Tejgyan Projects (Value Education, Women Empowerment, Peace Initiatives)

TGF undertakes projects to elevate the level of consciousness among students, youth, women, senior citizens, teachers, doctors, leaders, organizations, police force, prisoners, etc.

Now you can register **online** for the following retreats

Maha Aasmani Param Gyan Shivir
(5 Days Residential Retreat in Hindi)

Magic of Ultimate Awakening Retreat
(3 Days Residential Retreat In English)

Mini Maha Aasmani Shivir
3 Days (Residential) Retreat for Teens

🔍 www.tejgyan.org

Books can be delivered at your doorstep by registered post or courier. You can request for the same through postal money order or pay by VPP. Please send the money order to any one of the following two addresses:

WOW Publishings Pvt. Ltd.

1. Registered Office: E-4, Vaibhav Nagar, Near Tapovan Mandir, Pimpri, Pune - 411017

2. Post Box No.36, Pimpri Colony Post Office, Pimpri, Pune - 411017

Phone No.: 9011013210 / 9623457873

You can also order your copy at the online store: www.gethappythoughts.org

*Free Shipping plus 10% Discount on purchases above Rs. 300/-

For further details contact:

TEJGYAN GLOBAL FOUNDATION

Registered Office:

Happy Thoughts Building, Vikrant Complex, Near Tapovan Mandir, Pimpri, Pune 411017, Maharashtra, India.
Contact No.: 020-27411240, 27412576
Email: mail@tejgyan.com

MaNaN Ashram:

Survey No. 43, Sanas Nagar, Nandoshi gaon, Kirkatwadi Phata, Sinhagad Road, Tal. Haveli, Dist. Pune 411024, Maharashtra, India.
Contact No.: 992100 8060.

Hyderabad: 9885558100, **Bangalore:** 9880412588,
Delhi : 9891059875, **Nashik:** 9326967980, **Mumbai:** 9373440985

For accessing our unique 'System for Wisdom'
from self-help to self-realization, please follow us on:

happy thoughts	Website	www.tejgyan.org
YouTube	Video Channel	www.youtube.com/tejgyan For Q&A videos: http://goo.gl/YA81DQ
facebook	Social networking	www.facebook.com/tejgyan
twitter	Social networking	www.twitter.com/sirshree
(radio)	Internet Radio	http://www.tejgyan.org/internetradio.aspx

Online Shopping
www.gethappythoughts.org

Pray for World Peace along with thousands of others
at 09:09 a.m. and p.m. every day

Notes :

Notes :

www.ingramcontent.com/pod-product-compliance
Lightning Source LLC
LaVergne TN
LVHW041841070526
838199LV00045BA/1376